THE SEALS

The old man seemed to have relaxed his aggressiveness for the last couple of sentences, and now he sat brooding. In the silence Pibble looked round the room. It was like a photographer's studio set up for an advertisement of some appurtenance of gracious living – Cyprus port, perhaps, or Algerian cigars. All the props were there, the ranked books, the old oak tallboy and bureau, the smoky oil-paintings, rich rugs, glints of silver. But they were alien. The real room was the chill, clumsy, echoing stone, behind and above.

'Hey!' said the old man suddenly. 'Your foot's bleeding!'

Pibble stretched his stubbed toe clear of the habit. A blue-red ooze was trickling down its side.

'It doesn't matter,' he said.

'Yes it does, by George!' said the old man in a shrill shout. 'That's a damned good rug you're bleeding on – I won it off Rutherford in a bet in '23. Wrap it up in something.'

THE SEALS

Peter Dickinson

MYSTERIOUS PRESS

To Nils Gustaf Dalen –
who in 1912 was awarded the Nobel Prize for Physics for his invention of automatic regulators for lighting coastal beacons and other light buoys during darkness and other periods of reduced visibility.

THE SEALS

Mysterious Press books (UK) are published
in association with Arrow Books Limited
62–65 Chandos Place, London WC2N 4NW

An imprint of Century Hutchinson Limited

London Melbourne Sydney Auckland
Johannesburg and agencies
throughout the world

First published in Great Britain by
Hodder & Stoughton Ltd 1970
First paperback edition 1972 by Panther Books
Hamlyn Paperbacks edition 1983
Mysterious Press edition 1988

Author's Note
All the religion in this book is entirely imaginary,
and has no reference to any living God.

Printed and bound in Great Britain by
William Collins Sons & Co. Ltd, Glasgow

ISBN 0 09 941010 9

1

'You can see him now,' said the voice.

Pibble jerked up, the taste of his dream still pungent in his mind, though he could remember not one image that he'd dreamed, neither leaf nor syllable. His middle-aged heart was bonking its protest at the shock of this unnatural waking and levering up, but when he relaxed his head to where the quilted headboard should have been, chill stone prickled through thin hair. He willed his eyelids open; they fluttered up against the gravity of sleep, then clamped shut to seal out the desert glare. Through blinks he peered at his watch. It was just on three o'clock.

And the desert glare was only the fruity glow from the oil-lamp the woman was carrying. She held it high, as if she were modelling for the Statue of Liberty, so that her hand almost touched the rough vault of the cell.

Sister, um, Dorothy. Squat, stolid and unspeaking when Pibble had been introduced to her in the Refectory, but memorable for deep runnels that curved down her face from nose-corner to mouth-corner and gave her a look of implacable bitterness. She was the great man's keeper – Pibble could see him now, she'd said.

He twitched the harsh blankets aside.

'I'd've loaned you a pair of his pyjamas if you'd asked,' she said, managing at the same time to rebuke Pibble for not making a civilised request, and to imply that he was the class of person who always slept in his vest and pants anyway. Defensively he reached for his travel-weary shirt and the blue pin-stripe trousers whose knees were still splodged with white from the box of school chalks which he'd had thrust upon him in the helicopter.

'Don't you bother dressing,' she said. 'There's no time to waste. He gets tired after half an hour. I've brought you a habit. I'll wait outside.'

She put the lantern on the floor. As she went out her bare feet flapped against the paving like plaice on to a fish-monger's slab. Pibble sat on the edge of the bed and picked up the habit; it was as coarse as sacking, but dyed a fierce orange; he'd expected it to open down the front like a dressing-gown, but found that it was a simple tube cut, sleeves and all, from one piece of cloth – a garment only a degree less primitive than a shawl.

He wriggled into the tube like a woman wriggling into a nightie, then stood up to let the folds of sacking fall clear to his ankles; he was stooping for the lantern when he saw that the cowl was now dangling inanely under his chin, like a feed-bag, so there was nothing for it but to wriggle tedi-ously out, reverse the tube and wriggle in again. And the great man 'got tired' after half an hour. No time for shoes and socks, then. Pibble picked up the lantern and left. His own feet failed to reproduce the flapping noise that Sister Dorothy had made – she must put hers down with a peculiar vehemence, he decided.

She was waiting for him, stiff as a sentry in the salty dark.

'Sorry I was so long,' he said. 'I got it on the wrong way round.'

'They always do, first time,' she answered.

'Does the colour mean anything? The ones I saw on the Refectory were all green or brown.'

'Some bloody nonsense of Father Bountiful's.'

She flapped off up the short corridor and turned right into the cloisters. The pavement was numbing cold, and so uneven that he stubbed his toe twice before he reached the corner; he changed his pace to that of a man wading through shallow water, picking his feet up in a high arc so that he could put them vertically down instead of sliding them forward to collide with the inch-high cliffs which the amateur stone-masons had left. After his stumbles she was several feet ahead of him and striding into the blackness under the arches, knowing the way so well that her legs

6

adjusted without thought to every unevenness. Pibble held the lantern forward so that he could watch for further stumbling-blocks and waded after the blue-green habit which he could just see in the periphery of his vision. There was no chance to look out into the cloister courtyard and find what sort of a night it was, but he could hear the brisk westerly hissing along the slates and beyond that the deeper muttering of the sea. It was strange to hear none of the gulls which had obsessed the evening air when the helicopter had set him down; presumably even gulls must sleep. But not the wind, whose saltness smelt stronger in the dark; it was aseptic and romantic all at once, crying to his townee veins 'Love me!'

He felt that he could have walked twelve miles along starlit beaches, except that that would have meant walking three times round the island.

A man's voice spoke from nowhere.

'A fine night, Sister and guest,' it said. It had a Canadian accent as strong as Cheddar cheese.

Pibble jerked his lantern towards the voice. The man sat cross-legged in a nook in the wall, wearing nothing but a loin-cloth in the sea-chill night. Twenty years younger, Pibble might have achieved that posture for a few seconds before cramp gripped him; but it was clear that this man had already sat there several hours and expected to sit several more.

Brother Hope, his name was – one of the officers of the Community, brown-habited like the helicopter pilot. He'd played host to Pibble in the Refectory, apologising for the absence of the other . . . they had some cant word for their senior members . . . other . . . Anyway, there he had looked fat and stolid, laughing loud and often over their meagre meal. Now, stripped, his torso turned out to be meat and not fat, with muscles scooped and modelled like a bodybuilder's; and the brown eyes seemed sad in the lanternlight, and not foolish any more.

'Come on,' said Sister Dorothy from the dimness at the edge of the lantern's reach. 'I'm taking him to see him.'

The explanation was for Brother Hope; despite the drabness of intonation Pibble could hear the gamut of emphasis

7

that lay between the two pronouns – the first *him* being Pibble, a creature as negligible as a house-fly in an empty bedroom, and the second carrying the weight of a universe-filling deity.

'A OK,' said Brother Hope. His head fell forward until the bald spot in the centre of his scalp gleamed in the lamplight like a small moon. His lungs filled with tidal slowness. His stomach-muscles flicked into definition, moulded like wood-carving; no wonder he was in such good trim, if these were his normal exercises of contemplation.

'Come on,' said Sister Dorothy with the snarl of a mother whose child has loitered long enough at a pet-shop window. She strode round the corner of the cloisters. Pibble remembered how much of the precious half hour had already gone to waste; he scurried, forgot to wade, stubbed his toe viciously, stumbled among the hems of his habit, reeled helplessly forward and stopped himself from falling by hurtling against the far wall. The lantern went out with a crash and tinkle.

But when he recovered he saw that the world was not wholly dark. Sister Dorothy was standing in the faint light that came down the stairs below the great tower.

'I'm all right,' he gasped. 'I'm coming.'

She disappeared up the stairs. Limping and wading together, Pibble wallowed after her. The light came through a half-open door at the top of the first flight of steps; it seemed blindingly strong and steady compared with the faint flame that the lantern had produced. Sister Dorothy stood by the door in an attitude which showed that she expected him to go in, but would not do so herself. 'I'll sweep your mess up,' she said.

She shut the door behind him.

Sir Francis Francis still looked, at ninety-two, very like the photograph which Armstrong-Jones had taken of him nine years before, when he'd just come back from Oslo with his second Nobel Prize. Perhaps he seemed even hairier now, especially about the ears, but that was all. He wore a black jacket and pin-stripe trousers, and his Old Etonian tie was knotted round a starched white collar from which the neck, scrawny as a turkey's poked forth. Amid the round, prim, pink, myriad-seamed visage, the blue eyes blazed. He sat in a wing-chair by a crackling wood fire, hands crossed on an ebony walking-stick, and stared at Pibble as though he were the last creature on earth he wished to see.

'And who are you, sir?' he croaked.

'Pibble. James Pibble.'

'Then what are you doing in that tom-fool garment?'

'I was in bed. It seemed quicker than dressing.'

'Right. So you came. You cut it damned fine, hey?'

'I only got your letter yesterday – the day before yesterday, I mean. I caught the next train. You addressed it to Clapham, and we left that house before the war.'

'Always somebody living in one of those damned miserable little streets who knows where everybody's gone.'

'They forwarded it to the hospital where my mother died, and the hospital told them to try the rooms where I was living then, and those people sent it to my office.'

'Stop grizzling, man. I had to be certain of getting the right Pibble, hadn't I?'

'There aren't any others. I found some fish-merchants in the London Telephone Directory, but they spell their names differently.'

'Right. Willoughby Pibble, mechanic at the Cavendish Laboratory before the First War – what relation was he?'

'My father.'

'Thought so. Some malicious fellow sent me a newspaper cutting about you making a mess of your job, poking your nose in where it didn't concern you and causing a beastly rumpus. Just Will Pibble's style, I said to myself. Know what I'm talking about, hey?'

'Yes. My father worked for you at the Cavendish.'

'My personal mechanic. I didn't pay him, of course – couldn't afford to. We didn't call 'em mechanics, either. Dirty word then. We got 'em cheaper if we called 'em Research Assistants. Tchah! J.J. paid Everett out of his own pocket, but the rest of us had to squabble for the damned mechanics as if we'd been cockneys at a whelk-stall. Then your fool of a father attached himself to me, like a mongrel you pick up on a walk – scratch its damned ears for an instant and it follows you home. Bit of luck for him, choosing me, hey, considering who he might have latched on to – one of the Babus, f'rinstance or that American gel. Daresey he told you all about them.'

'He never talked about his time at the Cavendish. My mother sometimes did.'

'Your dad didn't see fit to tell me about *her*.'

'They weren't married until the war broke out; but they did their courting at Cambridge.'

'Damned good place for it.'

The old man seemed to have relaxed his aggressiveness for the last couple of sentences, and now he sat brooding. In the silence Pibble looked round the room. It was like a photographer's studio set up for an advertisement of some appurtenance of gracious living – Cyprus port, perhaps or Algerian cigars. All the props were there, the ranked books, the old oak tallboy and bureau, the smoky oil-paintings, rich rugs, glints of silver. But they were alien. The real room was the chill, clumsy, echoing stone, behind and above.

'Hey!' said the old man suddenly. 'Your foot's bleeding!'

Pibble stretched his stubbed toe clear of the habit. A blue-red ooze was trickling down its side.

'It doesn't matter,' he said.

'Yes it does, by George!' said the old man in a shrill shout. 'That's a damned good rug you're bleeding on – I won it off Rutherford in a bet in '23. Wrap it up in some-thing.'

'I'm afraid I left my handkerchief in my room.'

The old man snatched the blue silk triangle from his breast pocket and fluttered it in front of him as though he were saying good-bye to a steamer. Pibble hobbled across, took it and tied it round the bruised extremity.

'Carpet suffered quite enough from my damned bladder,' muttered the old man, 'without adding the effu-sions of your damned toe. Floorcloth in the coal-scuttle, water in that carafe on the spinet. Give the bloody bits a good soaking.'

Pibble took the cloth and the carafe, put them in front of the fender, knelt and began to swab. No amount of rehearsed conversations during that endless train-journey had prepared him for this. He dribbled more water on to the precious fabric. It was not, as a matter of fact, a very good rug – just an honest green-and-crimson Victorian affair, with a gothicised pattern. He glanced towards the fire to check how the pattern repeated and his eye was caught by a gleam under the brass fender – a large marble, except that the gleam came from a curved criss-cross of shiny wire – a shape he'd seen often before, though usually larger. A microphone.

'You whipped up here pretty damned smart, then,' said Sir Francis. 'What was the rush, hey?'

'You told me not to answer, but you said that if I hadn't come by the last Tuesday in March you'd assume I wasn't coming. That's today. I didn't even have time to go home and pack.'

'That's the spirit, young fellow. Yours not to reason why. Drop everything and come when I whistle. Leave the students to burn London, hey? You must have thought it damned important?'

Pibble stopped swabbing and stared at the unwinking gadget under the fender. It was bad enough answering the sneering old voice above his head; why should he pour these privacies out for a tape-recorder, or for the ear of some holy eavesdropper?

'My father died when I was eleven,' he said slowly. 'My mother lost her memory during the Second World War. She often spoke of him before that, but she was a very religious woman and her religion tended to colour her account of him. I have never been able to find anyone else who knew him well, but I want to know everything I can about him – I can't explain why. Anyway, his dealings with you seem to have affected his whole life and . . .'

'And I might be dead any moment, hey?'

Pibble said nothing. The creaking voice paused; when it went on it was in a lower tone, oddly secretive, as though the old man had his privacies too.

'Wondering why I sent for you, I daresay,' it said.

Pibble picked up the carafe and tilted it sideways under the fender.

'Hey, what are you up to, you damned fool?' said Sir Francis. 'You don't need that much water.'

Pibble carefully eased the fender upwards until he could pour the remains of the water directly into the microphone, which crackled and spat. He had occasionally been involved in eavesdropping operations at the Yard, without ever feeling quite happy that this was a policeman's proper work. Ruining this nasty toy salved that faint guilt. When he looked up the old scientist was grinning like a gargoyle.

'Any more of those, hey?' whispered Sir Francis.

Pibble stood up and nosed round the leather-smelling room. He hadn't much hope of spotting a professionally installed mike, but the one he'd spoiled had been so clumsily hidden that he thought he ought to be able to find another flex, at least. He was looking behind the pictures when he remembered how crazily thick the masonry of the tower was: the wires would have to come in through an existing opening – yes, the flex for the first one ran from the fireplace under the carpet and then sneaked out round the jamb of the door, as inoffensive as a sleeping snake. There was nothing at the window.

When Pibble turned back the sage was coming out of the small door in the further corner of the room, carrying a toothmug full of water. He made quavering signs to Pibble, who lifted the fender up and propped it on a square of peat so that there was room to slide the toothmug under it and immerse the whole microphone.

'Damned stuff, electricity,' said the old man, as though he were cursing an eccentric stable boy. He sank carefully back into the wing chair.

'Know *how* it works,' he said, 'but never know whether it *will* work, hey? That damned gadget might dry out and be functioning right as rain in thirty seconds, or it might be spitchered for ever. I've spent weeks – months – of my life trying to make some damned apparatus work. Design first class – done it myself. Workmanship first class – sacked the men if it wasn't. Micromagnetometer once, early days, near drove me loony till I spotted one brass screw in a steel frame generating its own charge. Where were we?'

'You were asking if I had any idea why you sent for me. I

12

imagine it had something to do with your book – you wanted to put in a footnote about my father, perhaps?'

Sir Francis's voice dropped from a creak to a croak.

'What book are you blathering about?' he said.

'I saw some extracts from your memoirs in one of the Sunday papers. The introduction said that you hadn't quite finished, and that you were working backwards.'

'You're thinking of someone else, you damned fool.' The voice was back to its normal level of unsuppressed arrogance, making it clear that only a buffoon like Pibble would confuse the memoirs of Sir Francis Francis with those of some come-lately hedge-scientist. Pibble gazed at his blue-swathed toe and collected his thoughts: it showed you how cut-off from the world Clumsey Island was, the old man thinking it possible that anyone, let alone Pibble, should make that mistake. The book – or rather the Sunday paper extracts – was unconfusable with anything. 'The publishing event of the decade,' Pooter had called it in *The Times*. 'All the dirt and all the knowledge. Lytton Strachey cross-bred with Bertrand Russell.' The first instalment had borne that out.

'The piece I read,' said Pibble slowly, 'was about your time, helping to build the first atom bomb.'

'My dear man,' said Sir Francis, 'there were several hundred garrulous prima donnas down there, and every damned one of them's written his memoirs.'

'There was a long section in the piece I read about the sexual habits of some of your American colleagues. I remember a bit about one physicist – they didn't print his name – who was trying to arrange a divorce with his wife, but they were so determined not to be commonplace that they used to meet and invent plausibly ingenious forms of cruelty which she could allege against him, and then the imaginary details so stimulated them that they invariably ended the session in bed together. I haven't read about *them* in any of the other books.'

'Rubbish!' shouted Sir Francis. 'Everybody knew them. He was a damned priggish Bostonian, but she was one of those fleshy New York Jews who lean their tits against you while they tell you how their marriage is coming apart. Her

13

breath smelt of melons.'

'The paper printed a page of the manuscript,' said Pibble. 'You could see it had been photographed, but was quite clear, and just the same handwriting as your letter to me. There was a long word crossed out near the bottom of the page.'

He looked up from his bandaged foot to find the harsh eyes staring at him, so exophthalmic now that they looked as if they might pop out and roll across the carpet. And the cheeks had lost their unnaturally healthy pink and become mottled with purple.

'Are they stealing something you *have* written or forging something you haven't?' said Pibble.

'I've written the damned stuff,' croaked Sir Francis. 'Who're they, hey?'

'Who are who?'

'Damned fellows cribbing my book, you fool. What are you going to do about them?'

'Me?'

'You're a peeler, a'n't you. Arrest them!'

'I imagine that at least some of the people in the Community must be involved, except that none of them seem to be very interested in money. I can't imagine any other motive.'

'Everybody's interested in money. I know. I've been poor, and then rich, and now I'm poor again. My book's worth a packet of money, what's more.'

'They must have known you'd find out.'

'Not a bit. No damned papers on the island, no wireless either, not counting the radio telephone.'

'But people would write to you, surely. People you used to know?'

'Not sure I've been getting all my mail lately.'

'Was that why you told me not to answer your letter?'

'Course it was, you damned ninny. Spring you on them and see. How much of my stuff did they print?'

'Only one extract has appeared so far, but the introduction implied that several more were coming and that the book would be out in the autumn. It seems a long time to keep it secret from you. But I suppose the thieves might be content to take the money from the newspaper extracts and the advance on the book and clear out. Even so, it was a hideous risk, I'd have thought – the sort of thing only a simple-minded thief would try. The *Sunday Times* was badly had a couple of years ago over some forged Mussolini papers; I can't imagine that any of them would print your stuff without some fairly water-tight authorisation from you.'

'Never mind that,' snapped the old man. 'Here's another damned fishy thing. Why did you drown that microphone, hey? I might have popped it there for my own good reasons, mightn't I?'

'I thought of that,' said Pibble. 'But I was fairly sure that something, well, unusual was up. Your choice of this hour in the morning to see me, for one thing, when everybody else is likely to be asleep; and your not having told the helicopter pilot to expect me; and your writing to Clapham when you could have written to Scotland Yard and simply asked if I was the right chap – it still seems a roundabout way of getting hold of me (in fact you nearly didn't); and the indirect way you talked about my job when I first came in – I thought it meant that you didn't want to parade my connection with the police.'

'Damned claustrophobic little streets,' grumbled Sir Francis, 'with their yellow bow windows and stained glass in the porches. Nobody moves out of them for generations. I've already told you someone was bound to know where you'd got to. Do I have to say everything twice? Or don't you trust me, hey?'

Trust the family traitor? Pibble said nothing.

'Your dad did,' said Sir Francis. 'And he was always jumping to conclusions, just your style. What're you going to do about my book, Pibble?'

'How many copies are there?'

'No copies. Write it all out in my own fist – damned good hand I've got, too.'

Pibble remembered the spiky copperplate of the letter now in his wallet – back in his cell, where anybody could sneak in and inspect it – not that it told anything, and besides he'd already had to show it to the helicopter pilot.

'And you've still got the whole manuscript here?' he said. 'Are there any bits missing?'

The old man grunted out of his chair and hobbled spryly across to a black, squat bureau, where he unlocked a drawer with a key from his watch-chain. He lifted out a swadge of foolscap, ruled with faint blue lines and covered from top to bottom and margin to margin with the same quick and careful script – so like every other gentleman's hand of sixty years ago, so different from most of them in its tough self-certainty. Even at ninety-two he formed each loop without a quiver. Pibble peered over his shoulder.

'Four-fifths finished,' said Sir Francis. 'Been doing the bits which amused me first. Scared that some of the ninnies I worked with would die on me before they could read what I said about them.'

He rustled through the pile with the sureness of a rabbit scuttling through its home copse; and the pages seemed as haphazard as the least tended copse in England: the folios were numbered, but not in any order, and there was a galaxy of starred cross-references.

'Bother is,' said Sir Francis, 'writing's so damned one-dimensional. Begin at the start and follow the thread to the end. But life a'n't like that – not *my* life . . . here we are. This the bit you saw?'

Pibble scanned it through.

'They cut the part about Linus Pauling,' he said. 'I don't think it's actually libellous –'

'Tom-fool law,' interrupted Sir Francis.

'. . . but they might have thought it was bad taste, I suppose.'

'Stick to the point,' snarled Sir Francis, 'and stop waving your damned bourgeois sentiments under my nose. If your toe's stopped bleeding you can give me back my hand-kerchief. What are you going to do about my book, hey?'

While Sir Francis nudged the pile of manuscript back into its drawer Pibble sat down by the fire and removed the blue silk. It wasn't bleeding, and wasn't even very badly bashed – he wouldn't lose it. Forty years ago Miss Fergusson, daughter of a bishop, making a few precious shillings a week by giving dancing lessons to the children of shopkeepers, had called him 'The Pibble who has no toes.' Surprised that he hadn't forgotten her, he stared vaguely at the fire. The Community, however impoverished, must value their prize convert highly if they imported logs to this treeless isle for him to burn among the uninspiring peat. And giving him electricity too: that meant there was a generator somewhere. He was all right, and if some villain was nicking his precious manuscript he'd be discovered in the end. The old boy still had plenty of life in him, and Pibble owed him nothing. Nothing.

'You asked me whether I trusted you,' he said. 'And before that you asked me what motive I had for dropping everything and rushing up here. I don't get the impression that *you* trust *me* either, and if so . . .'

'I trust you all right, you damned stupid nincompoop,' shouted Sir Francis, 'provided you don't try to do any thinking for yourself.'

'You trust me because I'm a policeman?'

'Course not. Peelers are just as crooked as anyone else – more so, with their opportunities. I trust you, Pibble, because I knew your fool of a father. Tell you something: J.J. Thomson's personal mechanic, Everett, was a first rate glass-blower, so he made most of the vacuum flasks we used in the Cavendish, for storing liquid air, mostly. He was chums with a rich little tobacconist, who spotted a nifty chance for making a fortune. Tobacconist offered Everett half-share in a business making vacuum flasks for the public – just the thing for taking your tea out for a picnic, keeping it hot, hey? Cracking good scheme, you'd have thought, but Everett turned it down. Vacuum flasks, he said, were not for the likes of ignoramuses out for Sunday larks on the Cam – they belonged to the Laboratory. Stuffy as all-get-out he was about it, prating about his duty to J.J. when he could have pocketed a million quid. Very intense relation-ship some mechanics built up with their masters. Why, *you* came haring up here, young Pibble, to find out about your damned dad, dead these forty-three years – and your dad would have stayed in that shocking little house, just in case I sent for him. That's why I trust you. Help me back to my chair.'

He was swaying on his stick by the locked bureau, looking frailer all of a sudden. Pibble went across, took him by the arm and guided him back, settling him in the pose in which he'd first found him. He got no thanks.

'Main point is,' said Sir Francis, 'I've not shown that stuff to a soul, not even Dorrie. But it's been nabbed by some scoundrel and sold to a common Sunday rag.'

'My father . . .' said Pibble.

'Shut up, man – I'm going soggy any minute – I can feel it coming. Dorrie'll bring you back in three hours forty minutes and you can tell me who you've arrested.'

'It's the middle of the night.'

'Very likely. Now send Dorrie in – she'll be waiting outside.'

'I shan't find anything out at this hour of the night.'

'Oh, go away and leave me alone. Can't you see I'm tired?'

The change had been quite extraordinary in its speed: from the clan chief of the highlands of the intellect to this whining elder. Sir Francis watched dully as Pibble lifted the microphone out of the tumbler, removed the log, settled the fender into position, carried the tumbler back into the bleak little bedroom, returned the carafe and floorcloth to their proper places, and left. Sister Dorothy, in her sentinel stance, was waiting for him at the top of the stairs.

'Is he all right?' she hissed.

'I think so. I left when he said he was tired.'

'You've kept him ten minutes longer than usual.'

It was an accusation. She handed Pibble the lantern and went through the door without another word.

It was hard to walk downstairs with a natural gait while following the flex by the yellow dimness from the wick; luckily the amateur stonemasons had done their work so unevenly that a certain amount of stooping and peering seemed plausible. The flex turned the corner at the bottom of the steps in the direction of Brother Hope in his alcove. Along the flat Pibble was forced to move faster, but a carefully timed stumble allowed him to stoop close enough to see that it still ran along the right-angle where the paving joined the wall. Then it snaked up into the alcove.

'Excuse me,' said Pibble. 'I'd like to go out for a short walk. Is there anywhere I mustn't go?'

Brother Hope emerged like a snail from the shell of his trance, with a slow, blind hesitation.

'Pardon?' he said.

'I'd like to go for a short walk. Is there anywhere I mustn't go?'

'. . . a naughty boy to get so excited,' said a strange, cooing voice out of nowhere. Sir Francis's querulous creak got as far as 'I'm all . . .' before Brother Hope appeared to scratch his buttock and cut him off.

'The island's yours, and God's,' said Brother Hope. 'Make yourself at home.'

'Thanks,' said Pibble, and walked on. The flex naturally no longer ran along the wall, Damned stuff, electricity, for the microphone to dry out and function perfectly at the moment he was opposite the alcove – Brother Hope must have a lowish opinion of policemen if he didn't expect Pibble to guess that something was awry. Wrong – they didn't know he was a policeman. Even so, for verisimilitude's sake, he'd have to go for his walk, though his neck was aching for the pillow. As he turned the next corner of the cloisters a soft shape fluttered out from the arches, thin arms coiled round his neck and the corner of his jawbone was kissed so fervently that he could feel the slimy hardness of teeth against his unshaved skin.

The kissing stopped.

'I am more than gratified that Your Highness was able to come,' said an ultra-genteel female voice. Pibble raised the lantern from the folds of his habit so that he could see who was draped so living-warm, and so garlic-smelling, against him. Black hair, a death-pale oval face – seventeen, perhaps – with a strange, small mouth drawn down into an even stranger smile, the upper lip quite straight and the lower lip bowed so deep that all the gums showed. The girl wore a habit the same blue-green colour as Sister Dorothy's. Suddenly she disentwined herself and drew back so shrinkingly that Pibble was at once steeling his nerves against the coming scream.

'Your Highness is displeased with my poor hovel,' she

19

said in a faint voice.

'Not at all,' said Pibble emphatically. Then, feeling that he ought to explain the stolidity of his response to her welcome, he added 'It's a cold night.'

'Pardon me,' twanged a deep voice behind him. Brother Hope surged out of the darkness, now wearing the brown habit he had worn in the Refectory.

'One of our servants,' explained the girl rapidly. 'They are all desperately loyal to the Cause, I do assure you.'

'Meet Sister Rita, Superintendent,' said Brother Hope at the same time. 'Why, Reet, you've certain-sure trodden on a big snake to-night. Let's take you home to Sister Charity.'

The fat hand looped out from the brown folds, took the girl by the elbow and swung her effortlessly round. Brother Hope's nod over her shoulder meant, as plain as speaking, that Pibble was expected to take the other elbow and march her back to quarters. But before he could make up his mind which side he was on, or even recover from the mild shock of finding that Brother Hope *did* know he was a policeman – knew the exact rank, in fact – the girl slipped her arm through his and leaned her head on his shoulder.

'Come,' she said softly. 'This good fellow will show us the way.'

'Which square were you on, Reet?' said Brother Hope impassively.

'Your Highness will find the dialect a trifle quaint,' said the girl. But she spoke with a degree less certainty, like an actress who knows she has forgotten her next cue.

'Can you count the hairs on your own head, Reet?' said Brother Hope.

The girl gave a high, social trill of laughter. Then she shook herself, altered her minuet-like pace to a mousy drifting, drooped her head submissively and said, 'Only God can count the hairs of His own head.'

If Pibble had been listening out of sight he wouldn't have known it was the same woman speaking. She had two voices. Brother Hope dropped his hand from her elbow and she walked on unguided.

'Can you count the sins of your heart, Reet?' said Brother Hope in a tone so conversational that he might

20

have been asking her about her holiday in Torquay.

'Only God can count the sins of His own heart,' said Rita. 'And He has none.'

'And he has none,' intoned Brother Hope. 'What do the stones say to your feet, Reet?'

'The Prince has given me such beautiful gold sandals,' said Rita in her other voice. 'I am to wear them to the Cardinal's ball.'

Brother Hope sighed in the dark.

'That was some snake you trod on to-night, Reet,' he said sympathetically. 'You'll need plenty ladders to work back to your old square. Good-night, Superintendent. This is as far as we go together. That gate yonder won't be locked. I'll see Reet back to Sister Charity.'

He nodded affably and swung the girl off down a passage. Pibble walked on over the erratic paving, trying to remember something from Police College refreshers about schizophrenia. The schizos he'd met in the course of his job had mostly not been the harmless ones, but had worked out their fantasies of power or vengeance on their fellow-citizens.

The rough timber of the gate was badly hung and scraped open in jerks. He stared into the wind-possessed dark and wondered about his own mind: what complex of oppression and ill-luck would split that cunning bauble into two halves? Would he crack easy? The bauble might be cunning, but he had a curious conviction that it was not strong, that there was a strain of broodiness in his blood. Mother (religion apart) had been as sane as home-baked bread until senility took over. But Father? A schizoid streak might explain the mysterious fracas at the Cavendish, and also the deliberate wasting of his talents in the Clapham booking-office. There had to be a reason for that, and also for Mother's acceptance of it.

The salt and icy air hissed through the coarse cloth of Pibble's habit as though the cloth wasn't there; he blessed Mary for her stolid belief in woollen underwear, but didn't dare mooch along the path. To keep what warmth he had he strode as briskly as he dared over the curious surface – except where an underlying rock projected it had been scraped or rolled quite smooth. Even so he held the lantern forward and walked in a hurried crouch, peering for obstructions that might batter his feet still further.

So who had stolen the manuscript, and why? And had they stolen it at all?

Ach, the hell with that – why had Sir Francis sent for him in the first place? Not for the book, apparently. Nor to find the thief, since the old man hadn't known of the theft until Pibble had told him. But there'd been that curious easing of aggressiveness when Pibble had said that Father never spoke about the Cavendish . . .

And the hell with that, too. His mind, too rebellious to think in an orderly fashion when it ought by rights to have been hull down in the seas of dream, kept sidling off from its proper problems back to a single obsessive figure, back to the quiet-voiced railway clerk who used to walk hand in hand with small Jamie Pibble along the streets of Clapham on Sunday afternoons, explaining things. Always explaining: the principles of the electric motor as a tram banged past; Lloyd George's betrayal of his soul and his party where a shredded election poster hung from black brick; natural selection when they came to the serried tulips in Councillor Blacker's front garden . . . Pibble, transfixed by the pang of memory, stood still and looked upward; the Atlantic wind was herding streamers of cloud so fast that the stars behind them seemed to be racing to the west – Father would have found that a fine occasion for an explanation of the phenomenon of parallax.

But what had he been *like?* How could anyone tell, who only knew him out of context – when his illness, and the war, and his row with Francis Francis had combined to cut him off from his proper sphere and leave him with no other concern than to keep his wife and son fed and warm in the cramped house on the steep street?

The only person who could answer that question had been dead forty-three years. (Odd that Sir Francis had bothered to count them.) He'd have known, too, whether he had schizoid tendencies. Pibble remembered the sleepless summer night when he'd crept down and settled on the canvas drugget which protected the precious stair-carpet, and then listened in a chilly half-dream to Father's voice as it explained the neighbours in terms of the cheap copy of *The Plain Man's Guide to Freud* which he'd spent his tobacco money on that week: why Betty Fasting made such a fuss about her dustbins; why Ted Fasting, in consequence, insisted on growing his prize onions in the front garden for all the street to see; why the Barton sisters held those hissing quarrels over the proper treatment of their aspidistra; why Joe Pritchett would cross the street to touch a lamp-post; and (just as mysterious to the shivering listener as any of the other explanations) why Mr Martin the rent collector – the one with the year-round snivel – ought to be watched in case he tried to become friendly with small Jamie. Father's even, earnest sentences hung disembodied in the dusk of the hallway, answered by Mother's interjections, shocked and admiring and commonplace. Small Jamie had fallen asleep against the newel-post and never knew how he was carried up to bed; Mother must have done it, for Father's lungs wouldn't have stood the effort. But he'd woken next morning knowing that Mr Martin with the bull's-eyes was somehow ogrish, though theirs was the only house in the street he didn't call at; small Jamie had worried for a week how to warn Sam Fasting (a whole year older, a whole year more worldly wise) without betraying his own secret knowledge – worried too long and decided too late.

Shrivelled with that childhood guilt Pibble walked on. The path, still smooth and rolled, sloped down and twisted to ease the sharp descent to the harbour. There was spume in the wind now that he was so close to where the big rollers picked irritably at the small granite protrusion of Clumsey Island, the ocean fingering this pimple of land. He'd only seen the island from above, peering through the windows of the helicopter at the tilting seascape as the machine swung and settled. Even to his unseamanlike eye, even through that grimy and half-opaque triplex, the harbour had seemed awkwardly placed, aimed due west into the gap below the Outer Hebrides where the main ocean came lolloping through.

The road yanked back on itself, running directly under

the cliffs; despite the scouring wind, Pibble could smell the unalterable smells of any harbour, however large or small, tar and diesel-oil and dead fish. He was walking along level and spray-slimy paving when two green lights blinked on in the dark before him, moved, and were eyes – eyes at the wrong level, too high for a cat and too low (please God) for a ghoul. He stood still and held the lantern forward.

The eyes were moving, becoming larger, nearer, a pony? But there was no clack of hooves – Crippen, it was a dog.

Stand still and don't be afraid, Father used to say. They can smell fear. So Pibble stood and sweated with terror as the creature stalked, hackles slightly raised, into his globule of lantern-light. He could see a faint brindling on its coat: it was a Great Dane. It stalked forward until its nose poked into his habit just below the nipples. There it stopped and snuffled.

The hackles dropped. Whatever it had smelt was not fear, evidently. It lowered its big skull and licked Pibble's free hand. He scratched it behind the ears, then walked a few yards along the quay until he came to a bollard, on which he sat. The dog plonked its head into his lap, nuzzling his arm for more attention. Pibble settled the lantern on the stones behind the bollard and tried to see into the dark. The total blackness behind him was cliffs, and the squatter blackness to his right was a large shed. Straight in front the gleam of starlight flicked off the crinkled water; where the movement ceased must be where the quay jutted out to give the harbour some protection from the booming ocean. But the quay seemed to bulge and give off a steadier glimmer in two places. Separating dark from dark to the west he discerned a probable horizon; following its line with his eye he saw that it was interrupted just where the lights gleamed by a small building, a building with masts, a boat.

He got up and walked along the quay, the dog pacing beside him, until his lantern showed him a white stern on which gleamed the gold word *Truth*. Bracketing this word two hulking outboard motors hung, swung up horizontally above the glimmering lop of the tamed ocean. A short gangway led to the deck and Pibble already had one foot on it when a wet and bony grip closed round his wrist and hauled him back.

It was the Great Dane, still very friendly, but urging him to desist for its own good reasons. Pibble allowed himself to be policed back to the bollard, where the hound immediately snuggled close against him, settling its heavy jowl into his shoulder almost exactly where Sister Rita's head had lain. The coarse hide quivered continually with the ecstasy of contact; Pibble, grateful for the animal warmth, put his lantern down again so that he could tease the long spine – four such beasts to adore him and he'd have been as cosy as any nightwatchman over his brazier.

Think, Pibble! He wanted you up here for something, and he was uncertain how much you knew. Just an old man's whims, perhaps – senility can take other forms than the ones you once became so drearily familiar with. But (a) there is a probability, at least, that a valuable document has been pirated, and (b) you don't know quite whose pigeon it would be, but surely the Community is the wrong place for a schizophrenic like Sister Rita.

He shuddered like a labourer shaken by his road-drill.

Poor Pibble, trying to tune in to sense and duty, those stodgy inescapable angels, telling him to find out what he could without causing a disturbance, then go home and make a report which would send some colleague round to ask questions at the newspaper office and publishers, and another to come winging up to Clumsey Island to disrupt the monks' harsh idyll – but through the signal came a mush of other voices, as happens at night, saying but then how'll you ever find out what did happen at the Cavendish? Only the old man can tell you, the last witness, sick, compos only at the regular four-hour intervals when the fierce mind spouts regular as a geyser – and he's cheating you over something, as he cheated Father over something, but you've a counter to bargain with, being a policeman and trying to trace the supposed memoir-stealers, hey?

Father, told these motives, would have bent his index finger back, paled, made a false start, and then shown small Jamie in quiet phrases too clear for any misunderstanding that he was lying to himself, cheating himself. 'Get the

25

half-crown accent!' the coalmen had jeered when Father went up the street to tell them that they were giving the Miss Bartons short measure, but small Jamie, even now, had no such counter-attack.

So he should make a report. It should cover both the manuscript and the Community effect on Sister Rita and other fragile minds.

A single midnight meeting with one near-senile elder, and another with a crazed teenager? Some report! Oh yes, and the microphone.

Pibble stared at the harbour and found that he could follow the quay out to the blind light-tower at its end. Craning round he saw that the sky above the cliffs was paler, and the stars diminished. Could it be drawn already? The hound sighed as he rose, but did not follow him up the cliff path into the wind's inimical caress. So at least it would be tolerably honest to rootle around for a day or two more; and he'd need an excuse for staying, which Sir Francis would have to supply by pretending to wish to know more about the Pibbles for his book; and that would mean several more interviews in which the talk would run, inevitably, on Father.

It wasn't dawn, it was moonrise. Hard to connect this indifferent crescent with the dreamy, rust-tinged round that shines on Lovers' Lanes. It was well up in a big patch of clear sky, just to the left of the buildings; so silhouetted the central tower looked crookeder than ever. Even this theatrical light, enhancing the gaunt outline while concealing the muddle and mess of the lower buildings, could not lend the structure a momentary dignity. It was certainly big – a gruesome amount of human effort had gone into building it – and would be vast when it was finished, if ever. Pibble had a momentary vision of the entire island covered with this quasi-Gothic fungus. But its confused proportions disguised its size. It reminded him in some ways of those strange, isolated sheds which Air Force engineers improvise on the perimeter of airfields, in the nastiest available brick, with the ungainliest conceivable outlines, on the most conspicuous skyline, and then top off with a rust-dribbling water-tank.

But now it meant sleep and warmth, if there was warmth anywhere in the world. Pibble tramped gingerly towards it. Either he was becoming cannier at walking without shoes or his feet had lost all feeling.

2

'You can see him now,' said the voice again. 'You'll get the itch if you sleep in that bloody thing.'

Pibble knew that he hadn't slept, but how had he been so anxiously fishing for a sunken boat in Mount Pond on the Common, a grown man wearing a sailor suit which he mustn't get muddy? He opened his eyes.

There was no lantern this time. Drab daylight and icy air came through the glassless window.

'Don't wait for me,' he said. 'I know my way.'

'You excited him,' said Sister Dorothy, bitterly.

'He excited himself, I'm afraid,' said Pibble. 'Has he ever talked to you about his dispute with my father?'

'He doesn't talk to me now, about that or anything else. Try Brother Servitude.'

No time for shirt and trousers, but glorious socks, at least. Civilised shoes. Ouch! His left big toe was too swollen with last night's bruising to conform to the once familiar leather; and the outer edge of his right foot was very tender too. Socks alone, then? No. If he stole about like the rest of the Community there was an extra chance that they would forget to be on their guard, those who knew anything. Perhaps he ought to ask for a green habit, or a brown one – nobody else seemed to sport this staring orange. His skin was tingling strangely on his fore-arm, and he snatched back the sleeve to peer at a patch where the coarse cloth had printed its graph-paper squares on his sleeping flesh. Panicky with the dread of nameless blains and flakings, blotches and pustules, he started to wriggle out of the habit. And a finely inconspicuous figure he'd be, creeping about

29

Clumsey Island in blue pin-stripes on bare and bleeding feet. He wriggled back.

She was waiting for him after all.

'Don't let on that I told you,' she said, 'but you've got to remember he's not just old. He's ill.' Her voice was not quite as bleak as hitherto, but tinged with a faint echo of that cooing note which had come last night through the soaked microphone.

'He's a long way from medical attention, isn't he?' said Pibble.

'Brother Patience was a doctor,' she said. 'He gives him his drugs.'

'What's he on?'

'Cortisone.'

'Is that what makes him so . . .'

'Hairy?'

'No. I meant . . .'

'Bloody-minded?'

'I wouldn't . . .'

'He's always been like that, ever since I've known him, an utter bastard. Long before we came to this bloody place.'

'Why did you come?'

'He gave all his radio patents away to the Foundation, and we were broke. He used to come sailing up here, and I . . .Sh!'

She slipped him a not-in-front-of-the-servants glance as they came round the last corner. Brother Hope was still in his niche, apparently full fathom five in trance; not one puckering of gooseflesh showed on the smooth pink steppes of skin; apart from his shepherding of Rita he probably hadn't shifted all night from his original pose. He did not speak or stir as they passed. Pibble peeled off up the stairs, and Dorothy strode on without a word.

His nose told him before his eyes, but he was coughing in the reeking smoke of Sir Francis's room (sharp wood, rank rubber) before he could stop. A small gout of adrenalin gingered his middle-aged muscles up to the rescue of the doddering genius, supposing Pibble could find him in the murk.

'That you, Pibble?' cried the creaking voice from the far corner. 'Log fell out of my damned fire. Pick it up like a good fellow.'

'Are you all right?' called Pibble.

'Course I am, you damned fool. Get rid of that log. I'm in me bedroom.'

Pibble stepped back to the landing, took a deep breath and blundered across the room by memory. He could barely see the log, even when he was close to. It had fallen in the most peculiar fashion, neatly against the side of the fender; luckily the rug had been shifted since his last visit, so that wasn't burnt, nor the stone below – only the thin trail of flex which ran under the fender at that point and accounted for the burning-rubber smell. Pibble lifted the log with tongs and shoved it into the still cheery fire; then, weeping and blind, he plunged for the bedroom door. Who would have thought that one little log had so much smoke in it?'

Sir Francis, lagged with blankets, was crouched on the edge of the bed looking as out-of-context as a condor in a zoo. But the pop eyes were bright.

'Wire burnt through, hey?' he whispered.

'I couldn't see for smoke,' said Pibble, 'but I wouldn't have thought so. Only the insulation.'

'Damned rum thing, knowledge,' said Sir Francis. 'Here I am, full to the cruppers with knowledge – know more than anyone else in the world, I shouldn't be surprised. Ought to be able to dream up a hundred and one easy ways of putting a mike out of action, accidental on purpose, hey? Only thought of one, and damned inconvenient and damned fishy too.'

'Couldn't you simply send for someone and tell him to take it away?'

'Things a'n't like that, not like that at all. Leave the door open?'

'Yes, the smoke should clear pretty soon.'

'Find the beggar who's been cribbing my papers, hey?'

'Not yet,' said Pibble. 'I can't go around asking questions in the middle of the night.'

'But that's what the damned police always do,' objected

31

Sir Francis. 'Hoist you out of bed in the middle of the night, throw a blanket over your head and take you off to clink for questioning. Why can't you?'

'I haven't the authority.'

'Yes, you have – you've got mine.'

'I assure you, Sir Francis, I wouldn't be likely to get anywhere if I woke up Father Bountiful . . .'

'Couldn't do that – the damned incontinent maniac's nuzzling a half-caste actress half way up Everest. Rum end for the Hackenstadt meat millions, hey? Who's on the other end of the microphone?'

'Brother Hope.'

'Arrested him, then? He must be in it?'

'Probably, but not certainly. For instance, he knew I was a policeman and may simply have wished to know what I was up to, perhaps even to protect you.'

'Tchah!'

'If you want him arrested, I shall have to question him directly, then fly back to the mainland, make a report, persuade my superiors that the case is fit for investigation, clear our responsibility with the local police, and come back with a full-dress team with warrants signed by the local magistrates – and, I imagine, seeing it's you, about three hundred journalists.'

'Can't have that, you buffoon.'

'In that case I shall have to try and find out what's happened on my own, in an unofficial fashion. It's going to be difficult enough by daylight, without breaking into people's sleep.'

'Damned bore, sleep. I haven't slept for twenty-seven years, not counting anaesthetics.'

'I'm between jobs at the Yard, and I've got three days leave due to me. I could stay that long. The best cover would be to pretend that your relationship with my father and the episode at the Cavendish were more important for your memoirs than you, presumably, think they are.'

'Want to worm out all about your dad, hey?' said Sir Francis sharply.

'Certainly I'd like to know anything there is to know.'

'Vindicate him after all these years, o' course?'

32

'No.'

'I wouldn't waste a penny stamp to vindicate *my* father.'

'I'm afraid I don't know much about him,' confessed Pibble.

'No more do I. Boots is most of what I remember, stinking or rank black mud. He kept otter-hounds, went broke to feed 'em, had to take me away from Eton. Smashed up his son's education for a lot of damned smelly dogs.'

'That sounds an interesting chapter.'

'Not that sort of book,' said Sir Francis. 'Not about nobodies. My old man was a quintessential nobody – small country squire, kept otter-hounds, wife died in child-bed, only son too brainy to talk to, went broke, shot himself in a Vichy *pension*. Very low square, as my friends in the brown gowns would say.'

'How much are you part of the Community, Sir Francis? You don't wear the regulation dress, I see.'

'Tried it for a bit, got the itch, put myself back into gentleman's kit pretty damned quick.'

'But you subscribe to some of their doctrines?'

'Nothing to do with you, you damned peeler. But I'll tell you it's symbiosis, because you won't know what that means. Damned smoke gone, hey?'

Pibble rose and peered. The brisk wind had come bustling in through the open door and brushed the murk up the chimney. A faint tang of bonfires still hung among the bookshelves.

'It's quite clear,' he said over his shoulder, 'but I'm afraid I left the door open and it's pretty chilly.'

'Well, shut the door and poke the fire,' creaked the voice from the bedroom – a little louder, perhaps, than it need have spoken. Pibble obeyed, then carefully placed the poker across the bared inches of microphone wire and trod on it to make sure of a good contact. Sir Francis came in, hobbling under his blankets, peered at the poker, grunted and sat down in his chair.

'Silly thing to say, that,' he grumbled. 'Willoughby Pibble's son is certain to know what symbiosis means.'

'I think most people would,' said Pibble. 'There's a lot of

popular science about it these days.'

'Ought to be a law against it.'

'I take it that the Community has the kudos of having an immensely distinguished man among them, and you have some compensating advantage.'

'Great self-educators, these Pibbles.'

'But I'd have thought their actual creed was a little, um . . .'

'Your dad wouldn't have liked to hear his precious boy sneering at someone else's beliefs. Very steady chapel-goer, Pibble was. Very pi. Wouldn't even go down to the lab on Sundays to pump up my vacuums over the week-end – I had to do it. *Me!*'

'But he was an atheist,' said Pibble. 'Of course he had a very bad war and perhaps that . . .'

There was a brusque knock at the door, and Sister Dorothy stalked in carrying a large black enamel tray.

'I've brought two breakfasts,' she said with a sharp smile, 'so you didn't have to interrupt your chatter. Mrs Macdonald has smoked some more kippers.'

The smile stayed on her face, tense and secretive, as she set the tray on a small gate-legged table, slammed cutlery and crockery into position and slapped out, sniffing.

Pibble was unfamiliar with kippers. Poor as they had been between the rare patches of comfort, his mother would never have allowed such symbols of a working-class diet into the house. And now Mary, though she was some-times tempted by the eulogies of a colour-supplement chef out slumming, never bought the fish because it was 'tire-some'. He started to detach the backbone.

'No, no!' yapped Sir Francis from the other side of the table. 'Let me do it for you, you damned idiot! Slide your plate across.'

Pibble did so. The great scientist flipped the fish over, skimmed the skin off with three quick movements, then rapidly and gently teased the flesh away from the under-lying bones.

'Sure sign of a nincompoop,' he said, 'trying to eat a kipper that way up. Only met six people in me whole life who knew the right way – all the rest of 'em nincompoops.'

34

'I'd never tried before.'

'Poor man's food, hey?' snapped Sir Francis. 'You don't know what poverty means. You'd eat anything then, and damn your pride. Do the other one yourself, or mine will be cold.'

Pibble ate the smoky, tender, juicy flesh and studied the knack as Sir Francis did the same trick with his own fish.

'They're very good,' he said.

'Damned well ought to be. Caught in this sea and smoked on this island.'

'By the Community?'

'Course not, you fool. By the Macdonalds. Our lads wouldn't catch anything but dogfish, or if they did they'd cure 'em wrong, keep 'em wrong and cook 'em wrong.'

'I thought you had to smoke kippers with oak chippings.'

'Damned snobbery. Isn't a tree on the island. Our brown brethren fly in a few logs to coddle my old bones, but all the other fires are peat. Can't you taste it?'

The old man made a pyramid of the de-boned fish on his plate, reached for the salt-cellar and poured until the pyramid was as white as the Cuillins. Then he picked up a white pill from the tray, put it on his tongue, frowned, and washed it down with tea.

'Damned waste of good food,' he said sourly as he began to demolish and eat his snow scene. Suddenly, for the first time in forty years, Pibble remembered the lodger who had come to stay with the Barton sisters, to the thrilled scandal of the street, though they were well past fifty – a tall lethargic man with a strangely darkened skin, who used to fall asleep sometimes in the middle of conversations. He'd done just that trick, piling already salty food with mountains more salt, then eating the mess without relish. Four months he'd stayed, a mooching centre of melancholy, before he was taken off to hospital. He'd been a gentleman, the Bartons had explained, but there was something wrong with his glands. The word 'Atticus' dodged into Pibble's consciousness, probably by word-association with attic salt.

'Rum thing,' said Sir Francis as he finished gobbling. 'Your dad would have swooned with joy at the idea of

35

breakfasting with me, and now you sit there as suspicious as a peasant at a law-case.'

'Was he any good at his job?' asked Pibble.

'It's a contract,' said the old man after a pause. 'It's a bore, but it's a contract. You find out who's been cribbing my papers, and in return I'll tell you every damned thing I can remember about your miserable father. Though I've a good mind to report you to your superiors, blackmailing me this way.'

'It's up to you,' said Pibble. 'If you want me to do the job on my own I must have an excuse for staying here. Even then I can't guarantee results. It would be much quicker and more efficient to go through the regular channels, bring in detectives with an official status, who could ask straightforward questions, take fingerprints and so on.'

'Can't have that,' said the old man.

'Why?'

'Mind your own damned business. You're a fool, Pibble. No wonder the crime rate's rising. All you've got to do is show an interest in their idiot beliefs, drop a hint or two that you feel like enlisting. The moment they see a chance of getting you out of that orange nonsense into a green one, they'll beg you to stay.'

'What do the colours mean?'

'Ha! Brown's for earth, rock and stone. Green's for growth and hope and that kind of nonsense. That orange number you're sporting signifies the everlasting bonfire which will gobble up the good citizens of Babylon. I got to know the jargon damned well, one time. But you ask *them* that sort of question to start with, and they won't care what you ask after.'

'Questions about you and your papers?'

'Any questions at all, provided you put 'em right. *Course* you're nosey about me – that's why half the idiots come here in the first place – I'm the prize catch. You don't think they'd expect you to be interested in anyone else in the island, hey?'

'They know I'm a policeman already.'

'I'd have thought that's a thing you'd keep under your hat.'

'All I said was that I was a civil servant. But one of the brothers called me Superintendent last night, after I saw you.'

'No odds. Everyone expects peelers to be half way to Colney Hatch. They'll think you came to spy, remained to pray, hey? That won't surprise them; why, their top thinker was a Gunner. You start with him – he's a damned garrulous ninny with a footling moustache – in here at all hours prattling away – I like him. Start him off and he'll tell you everything. Larky do if he converted you, hey?'

'I'll try to keep my end up.'

'Having no beliefs gives you no defence, young Pibble. What sort of pap did your irreligious dad feed into you?'

'He was an atheist, but not aggressive about it, and my mother was very serious about her religion. So he left it to her to send me to Sunday School and so on.'

'And landed you with half a God and a few crumbs of creed, hey? Much good they'll do you once our brown brothers start work. My dad did better by me, at least – he spoilt everything. I believe in *me*.'

'You never told me how good at his job my father was,' said Pibble.

'Persistent little terrier, a'n't you? Your father was a fair run-of-the-mill mechanic, and a damned good glass-blower. Trouble was, he never learnt his place. First, he wasn't contented with working for the Lab in general – he wanted to be somebody's personal mechanic – mine – like Everett was J. J.'s. Next, he wanted to *think* about what I was doing, make suggestions, join in. Always borrowing my Journals to read, then coming back and asking damn-fool questions which showed he'd worried some theory out and got it all wrong. I couldn't choke him off, because I needed him. Didn't mind how late he worked for me, provided it wasn't Sunday. J.J. never liked keeping the Lab open late, mark you – said we couldn't afford the electricity. Your damned dad, Pibble, was the only man in that Laboratory who could blow me vessels big enough to play with my gas plasmas, if I wasn't going to go crawling to Everett, or to Fred Lincoln with his waxed moustache and his big bum – and *then* I'd have to wait a fortnight. So I had to

37

put up with his impertinent fool suggestions – and all the time, remember, knowing that he was earning more as a mechanic than I was. Me, the best mind of my generation, drudging along on a Readership worth forty quid a term, a hundred and twenty damned pounds a year.'

'Could you live on that?'

'I couldn't, but I did. You saved out of your scholarship when you were an undergraduate. Not so hard for the others – clerks' sons from places like Sheffield – see the class of company my dad had condemned me to – but I'd been at Eton, and had to stand on Magdalene Bridge and watch a ninny I'd been at school with hacking off to Cottenham Races leading a hunter which'd cost him more than my whole year's savings. Ninety quid a year I got when my scholarship ended, Demonstrator at the Cavendish Laboratory and supposed to be proud of it. There we were, nosing out the knots the stuff of the universe is tied together with, on ninety quid a year. If one of us was offered a job elsewhere he'd glare at us and neigh – damned strange voice he had, and loose false teeth – 'What are they paying you? Thousand a year?' as though we'd have to be *bought* to leave the Cavendish. And he was right, too. So we lived on our savings and our pittances – and mark you, if I'd been shifty enough to mug up a bit of Latin and take orders my college could have found me a living out Ely way worth fifteen hundred – and when our savings ran out we left, or we starved. I starved.'

'I'm glad my father was some use to you.'

'Your dad was a damned inconvenience, glass-blowing apart. Did he ever blow glass for you?'

'For me?'

'Lab mechanics are simple souls, Pibble. If they've got kids, they blow glass for them, make little knick-knacks, which the kids bust in ten minutes and cut their damned fingers on the bits. All my dad ever blew for me was bubbles of stinking black mud, out of the tops of his boots as he squelched across the hall.'

'I doubt if my father would have had the lungs for glass-blowing after the war. He was very badly gassed.'

'One talent, and he wasted it, hey? Now I've told you

whether your dad was any good at his job – you can show me whether you're any good at yours.'

'All right,' said Pibble. 'How long ago did you write the passage I read in the paper?'

'Last March. I've been scribbling for three years now – I don't do much at a shift, you know. Dammit, I'm *old!*'

'And not counting the time it was taken and copied it's been in that drawer all the time, as far as you know?'

'Of course.'

'You haven't left the island – for your operation, for instance?'

'Who told you about my operation?'

'You mentioned anaesthetics.'

'Jumping to conclusions, just like your fool of a father. I came here long after they cut me up, when I started on the book. Want to tell the world what I think of it before I die, hey?'

'If you don't sleep and you don't leave these rooms . . .'

'What do you take me for – a damned invalid? I stroll over to the Macdonalds' when the weather's half decent. They teach me Gaelic.'

'Did you go yesterday?'

'What's that got to do with it?'

'I wanted to know whether the microphone could have been introduced after I arrived. You took precautions that nobody should know I was coming, so if you didn't go out yesterday that means the microphone was put there before, and it wasn't only me whose talk with you they wanted to listen to.'

'Dorrie took me up to the shieling in the evening, seven-ish. The gels were out fishing before that.'

'I got here just after five. They showed me my cell and asked me to wait, which I did until supper, and then they took me back to my cell and said that Sister Dorothy would come and fetch me when you were ready to see me. Did you know I was here when you, er, came to at . . . it would have been eleven, wouldn't it?'

'Course I did, but I didn't feel up to coping with a mess of idiot questions then. I wanted to write.'

'I thought you were going to question me.'

'Ha! I know Pibbles. Get on with it, man.'

'Well, let's assume that they put the microphone in when you were out last night. They know I'm a policeman. Brother Hope is one of the senior members, and he was listening at the other end. You know the set-up better than I do. Could he be in this on his own, or would he be more likely to be acting for the whole Community? And if so, why? Are they short of money?'

'If I knew all that, you damned idiot, would I be asking you to find out?'

'May I have a look at the lock in the desk, please?'

'It's a good 'un. All college servants are thieves. Here's the key.'

The key fitted all the drawers. Each lock was a stolid brass affair, both intricate and tough, more than a match for the amateur picker; but down the inside rim of the second keyhole there was an extra brightness on one side, ending with a thin curl of swarf still attached to the main brass. No other scratches showed on the well-polished metal, and Pibble was unable to jiggle the key in such a way that it could conceivably have planed off that precise shaving. The lockpicking had been professional then, but far from artistic.

'Do many ex-criminals join the Community, Sir Francis?'

'How should I know, you nincompoop? You don't expect me to go hobnobbing with rapists, do you?'

'Well, I thought . . .'

'I'm tired, damn you. Can't you stop badgering me?'

Once again, with unpredictable suddenness, the note of senility had crept into the old voice. He seemed to have lasted longer this time – the result, maybe, of that monstrous helping of salt, and the pill; cortisone, presumably. Pibble stood up. 'I'll see what I can find out,' he said. 'Shall I come back in three and a half hours?'

'Damned fool,' said the old man lethargically, 'you won't find out anything. Do what you like, only go away. Dorrie'll be waiting outside. Send her in.'

But the landing was empty. The sentry had deserted her post.

'Who would not laugh if such a man there be?' Pibble asked himself as he went down the stone stairs. *

'Beg your pardon,' said Brother Hope, now in his brown habit, coming round the corner at the bottom.

'Who would not weep if Atticus were he?' said Pibble. 'It's just a bit of verse I can't get out of my head. Sir Francis asked me up here to talk about my father, and it seems to have stimulated my memory in odd ways.'

'Sure,' said Brother Hope. 'Brother Simplicity, we call him.'

And why hadn't this jovial yogi come bouncing in when the microphone failed? Well, a trance of communion with the infinite may be good cover for an eavesdropper, but the cover's blown if he snaps out of it too readily.

'He told me to send Sister Dorothy to him,' said Pibble. 'But she wasn't there.'

'OK, I'll find a guy to look for her.'

'You must be proud to have him here.'

'He's a good ad., right enough.'

Brother Hope wrapped his little cynicism in his gaudy laugh, just like any monk in any monastery who wishes to suggest how quaint it is that he should occasionally talk in the wicked accents of the world.

'You ready for breakfast, Superintendent?' he added.

'Yes, please,' said Pibble. It sounded a good chance to start asking questions, a time when it would be unnatural if he didn't appear inquisitive. But perhaps Brother Hope knew about the kippers.

'Breakfast's my main meal of the day,' he said.

'Sure,' said the monk. 'Follow me. The others are waiting.'

He strode off along the cloisters, light on his feet as a wing three-quarter. Pibble, scurrying beside him, at once banged his good big toe into a flagstone which rose a full inch above its neighbour.

'It's a remarkable building,' he said bravely. 'It'll be enormous when it's finished.'

'Twelve thousand furlongs each way, Revelation 21:16.'

'But isn't it supposed to be twelve thousand furlongs high, too?'

41

(Mother's sect had studied *Revelation* with great serious-ness.)

'Yeah. But maybe they're not Terran Furlongs. Brother Servitude is working on Father Bountiful's notes. Hi! Bruce, man!'

They were passing a place where an unfinished passage led outwards from the cloister wall. Crouched under the barrel vault, amid a powdery detritus of stone-chippings, a man in a blue-green habit was measuring a roughly squared boulder against a gap in the wall he was building. At Brother Hope's call he stood up and walked towards them, stopping under the cloister arch to make a deep oriental bow, palms together. Brother Hope answered in kind.

'Order a boiled egg for the guest, Bruce,' he said. 'Then find Sister D. and send her to the Tower Room.'

'Whose egg?' said Bruce in a dull voice.

'Make it Reet's. She trod on a mighty big snake last night.'

Brother Hope spoke with a salesman's cheeriness, but Bruce raised his eyes in solemn horror. When the glance would normally have looked level at Pibble it flickered away. Bruce dropped his tools with a clatter and darted off.

'Tuesdays we have oatcakes,' said Brother Hope, 'see-ing it's the third day of Creation. But if breakfast's your chief meal . . .'

'I'll be quite happy with oatcakes,' said Pibble hurriedly. 'I'd much rather not take someone else's . . .'

'Don't you fret about that,' said Brother Hope, smiling as a father might at a child's ineffective charities. 'Reet won't be eating to-day, not after last night.'

Hell, thought Pibble. Poor miserable girl. He felt a spasm of that raging nausea which cruelty-to-children cases always sucked up inside him. But a protest now . . . He stared at the fallen tools to distract his own fury. They too had been sadly mistreated: the mallet was no more than a small log, its bark worn smooth at the narrower end by Bruce's grip, and the other end a splintered mess. The cold chisel was a real tool, but a great bite was missing from its cutting edge. With implements like that, building the Eternal City would *need* eternity.

Brother Hope clucked for his attention, led him round the next corner and opened a door.

'Come in,' he said. 'Breakfast, it's just us Virtues.'

Pibble had expected to be taken to the Refectory where he had supped, but this was a small room, a white-washed barrel vault without ornament or detail. The air smelt pleasingly of mint. An old deal table, as from a farmhouse kitchen, ran down the middle. Some jugs and two big platters of oatcakes stood on it, and round it waited, standing, a dozen people in brown habits. Two were women. All, as the latecomers entered, made the same oriental bow. Before Pibble finished his gawky reply a stout little man rushed at him, hand outstretched in welcome.

'I'm Servitude,' he said, smiling primly beneath a tiny rectangle of moustache. 'We didn't meet last night, so you must come and sit between me and Providence. Here. Ready, Providence.'

The prodigiously bearded figure on Pibble's other side raised both arms towards the vault. A huge authority flooded the room.

'The sacrifices of God are a broken spirit,' he said. His voice was light and easy, but he sounded as though he meant it. Pibble found himself automatically joining in the response.

'A broken and contrite heart, O God, wilt thou not despise.'

That had been a favourite text at Mother's Tabernacle. Odd how all crank religions tend to shore their theologies up with the same baulks of Bible.

'He's having Reet's egg,' said Brother Hope from the other side of the table.

'First-class notion,' said Brother Servitude. 'Water, Superintendent? Charity tells us she trod on a snake last night.'

'Sure did,' said Brother Hope.

'Tsk, tsk,' said Brother Servitude. 'I won't introduce you all round, Superintendent, as you'll only get muddled. It takes training to distinguish between one virtue and another in the bad light of the world, eh? We had an emergency Council last night, or you would have got to

43

know us better in the Refectory.'

'Brother Hope looked after me very well,' said Pibble. 'I've been asking him about the plans for this building. Somehow I'd never envisaged the New Jerusalem being material – as material as granite.'

'Ah,' said Brother Servitude eagerly, 'that's a very interesting point, to which there is an equally interesting answer. The Papists aren't the only folk who can split a fine hair, you know. Now, when Adam created matter . . .'

'I'd forgotten about that,' said Pibble, late on his cue. Brother Servitude had paused for an interjection of surprise, but Pibble, unnerved by the total silence with which all the other Virtues were following what must be a familiar argument, had muffed his line.

'Oh yes,' said Brother Servitude. 'The old churches have been hushing it up for a long time. Ah, here's your egg – don't let it get cold. But if you look in Genesis you'll find there are perfectly clear accounts of *two* creations, one in Chapter One and one in Chapter Two. *And* they have different Creators, the first referred to in the Authorised Version as "God" and the second as "the Lord God", which was the best poor King James's bishops could do to differentiate between two totally different Hebrew words. Now, in Chapter One, verse twenty-eight, God created man in His own image, male and female created He them. Pass the salt, Providence – I'm afraid we don't get very fresh eggs on the island, Superintendent. None of that nonsense about using ribs to make Eve, you see. That comes later. But in Chapter Two, verse six and seven, we are told first that a mist went up from the earth and then that the *Lord God* formed man of the dust on the ground. Now that's as clear as daylight once you've spotted it. First of all man was created as a spirit – what else can God's own image mean? *Then* somebody else made man out of a material substance. They didn't have the philosophical abstracts that we have to express their ideas, of course, but what they meant by the mist was the spiritual fall of Adam – he no longer saw clearly, you understand? And that dust business is the creation of matter. It keeps happening.'

'Continuous creation, you mean?' said Pibble, because it

44

seemed his cue to flip a few words into the strange silence.

'Ha ha! Very good!' said Brother Servitude. 'I can see you've been reading your Fred Hoyle. No, no, no, though. We're dealing with metaphysics, not astrophysics. It's the material fall of Adam that keeps happening. Something similar has occurred on every planet which Father Bountiful has visited to date!'

'It can't be coincidence,' said Pibble.

'Ah!' said Brother Servitude, 'You hear that, Providence? He has the root of the matter in him!'

The monk on Pibble's other side turned his head. Something, a smile perhaps, stirred the forest darkness of his beard, but Pibble could see nothing except an improbable pair of eyes, pale as a single malt whisky, glowing. The strong gaze held his own for a moment, then Brother Providence returned to his oatcake. Pibble shivered slightly, feeling that he'd been visited from another planet, or perhaps another life.

'As you say,' said Brother Servitude, 'it can't be coincidence. There must be some larger plan, of which all this is merely a part.'

'How many planets has Father Bountiful visited?' asked Pibble.

'Twenty-seven to date,' said Brother Servitude.

'Twenty-eight as of March twelve,' said a Brother from the other side of the table. He had bruise-blue jowls and spoke with a heavy northern accent.

'You got a postcard last night?' said Brother Servitude excitedly.

'We did. It came on the helicopter with the Superintendent, but I couldn't read it in Council with Hope and Charity not there. How about now, Providence?'

'I don't see why not, Brother Courage.'

Brother Courage drew from the folds of his habit a bright postcard, whose picture showed peasants engaged in some traditional dance against a background of high peaks.

'He's still in Nepal,' he said.

'Mathematically the slopes of Everest are the ideal spot for planet-transference,' whispered Brother Servitude in Pibble's ear.

Brother Courage dropped his voice to a priestly register but failed to modify his vowels. ' "Fourth Planet of Gamma Scorpions",' he read, ' "Wish you were here. Planet entirely covered with water. Mile-high tides. Dominant race intelligent cuttlefish. Spiritual pattern as before. B. Hackenstadt." I'll pin a photo-copy on the board, of course.'

'Well,' said Brother Servitude, breaking with a gratified sigh into the long, glassy silence which followed, 'twenty-eight planets may not seem to you a very large statistical sample, amid the plethora of galaxies. But even were the choice between falling and not falling a simple either/or choice, uncomplicated by further options, twenty-eight planets in succession, without a single variant, represents odds in the neighbourhood of, let me see, a thousand million to one. Oatcake?'

'Thank you,' said Pibble, anxious to rub the nastiness of near-bad egg out of his mouth. 'You were going to tell me why it is proper for the New Jerusalem to be built of ordinary material stone.'

'Ah, yes,' said Brother Servitude. 'I'm afraid I got carried away. I don't often get the chance to talk to somebody from the outside world of your intelligence, Superintendent.'

Pibble, luckily, had his mouth full of oatcake, so was in no danger of being visibly aware of the slight chill of warning that breathed through the room. The oatcake was no more appetising than the egg; while the brethren were avoiding his eye he took the chance to slip it into his sleeve, and thence into the pouch at his waist. It was difficult to imagine how a reference to his own mild intelligence should disturb this holy, if manuscript-purloining, gathering, but Brother Servitude choked elaborately on a crumb and took a long swig at his mug before he gabbled on.

'The point is this – any Fall must be from a higher to a lower plane, for what else can the word mean? That is to say from a more real to a less real plane. We are all Platonists now, ha ha. So the things of our material world are in truth less solid, less substantial, than the things of that spiritual world. The more solid they seem to *us*, the more evanescent they will seem to the inhabitants of that world – lighter, more translucent, more exotic. This . . .' and he slapped the sturdy deal with his open palm '. . . would be rarer than topaz to *them*. You see?'

'I think so,' said Pibble. 'The ninth foundation was topaz, wasn't it?'

'Will be,' corrected Brother Servitude. 'But more important to our argument, the street of the City is described as 'as it were, transparent glass'. Or in my words, translucent.'

'The thing that astonished me,' said Pibble, 'is that you've found time to build so much. I'd have thought you'd have an effort merely to subsist on an island like this.'

Brother Providence's pleasant voice answered him from his other side.

'Wrong, I'm afraid, Superintendent. That was the error into which the mediaeval monastic communities fell.'

'The *physical* error,' interpolated Brother Servitude.

'Of course,' said Brother Providence. 'We who are sealed have been spared their spiritual errors. But the monks, Superintendent, all made the same mistake. They built their cloisters and chapels and dormitories, and they gardened and they prayed. But once they had completed their buildings they found themselves with time to spare. So they gradually complicated their simple discipline, and made it more and more luxurious. They grew nectarines. They praised their God in the invention of delicate sauces for carp. They decorated their manuscripts with images from the world they had theoretically renounced. Whereas we, a community whose discipline is to live with the utmost frugality we can achieve – we can concentrate on building. We have time to build for eternity.'

'You make it sound very, well, appealing,' said Pibble, studiously balancing doubt against enthusiasm.

This time the stir that ran through the room was different, like the tremor which runs through the spectators at a chess tournament when what had looked like a routine draw comes alive with a move that has not been fully analysed. Only Brother Providence seemed unaware of the change.

'If you are interested,' he said, 'I will show you over the Community later this morning. You may care to take a stroll round the island until I've finished my chores.'

'I went for a walk in the middle of the night,' said Pibble. 'I met the biggest dog I've ever seen.'

The Virtues, as if Brother Providence's mention of chores had been a signal, had clattered up from their benches and were beginning to troop out of the drab vault; but Sister Charity paused in the door, a smile suddenly flowering on the desert of her face.

'You met Brother Love?' she said. 'Isn't he *clever*?'

'Clever's the word,' said Brother Hope flatly. He took Sister Charity by the elbow and, without any apparent hustling, flicked her out of the room as deftly as a housewife flicks her husband's half-darned pyjamas under a cushion when the lady from Oxfam walks in unexpected. The brown habits swirled out of the door and Pibble was left alone with Brother Providence. This, he now knew, was the master of the Community, at least in Father Bountiful's absence. If the Virtues were collectively responsible for stealing Sir Francis's manuscript, here was the Top Villain.

'I suppose you are used to this,' said Pibble carefully. 'Everybody who comes here must be fascinated by what you are doing.'

The strange eyes watched him speculatively. The big head nodded in silence.

'I expect you find Sir Francis's presence a great attraction,' said Pibble. It was difficult to gush without gabbling.

'A great responsibility,' said Brother Providence.

'You mean you have to look after his affairs for him, and so on?'

Brother Providence looked hard at Pibble and ran his hand in silence down his beard.

'Consider,' he said at last. 'Here is this great soul, so near to going out, yet finding it so hard to throw the necessary number. And who knows what snake may not lie between him and the ultimate square?'

The eyes had lost their remoteness; below their surface it seemed as if something was glowing like a blown ember.

The beard, by concealing mouth and chin, made you concentrate on the eyes – an effect the opposite of that achieved by mid-winter sunglass-wearers. To rescue himself from incipient hypnosis Pibble studied the nose, an apparently boneless promontory so patterned by tiny veins that, but for the oatcake-and-water regimen of the island, he would have cast Brother Providence as a claret-and-snipe man.

'I'm glad Sir Francis sent for me,' he said, 'though it seemed an interruption at the time. People as old as that can be very demanding.'

'The newest stones are the softest,' said Brother Providence. 'They are naturally easiest to carve. It is the old, hard, weathered ones which are most rewarding. Shall we meet outside your cell in an hour's time, say?'

'Fine,' said Pibble.

'Just one other matter. Normally, the helicopter only flies on Tuesdays and Fridays, but if you wish to go and have finished your business with Brother Simplicity, I can arrange for you to be taken over.'

'Please don't. Sir Francis has a short attention span, and I'm trying to remember things which happened nearly fifty years ago, when I was a child. So we don't get a lot done at each meeting. I could go and come back, if that's what you want, but I'd much prefer to stay. Much.'

Overdoing it? To judge by the bearded monk's I-told-you-so nod, no. Standing, Brother Providence looked less large than he had sitting down, but no less imposing. His big face had implied a Friar Tuck torso; and indeed though his habit's folds now fell past no obesities, his stance suggested that his frame had once been used to supporting a greater weight.

'May I go anywhere I like?' said Pibble.

'Of course.'

'What I meant is that you must have one or two slightly, um, unstable characters in the Community, so I expect you have rules about things like the helicopter and the cliffs. I wouldn't like to break them.'

'The world you are used to – we call it Babylon – must be somewhat more melodramatic than ours, Superintendent.

49

You have been shown where the guests' toilets are?'

'Yes thank you,' said Pibble.

They walked out of the room to find the vault of the cloisters reverberating with a strange rhythmic grunting, but Brother Providence seemed to notice it no more than the ceaseless mewling of the gulls. He nodded and strode off over the uneven paving. Pibble walked more carefully in the other direction, and found the source of the noise round the next corner. Eight people in blue-green habits were hauling at ropes tied to a huge rough-squared boulder. It trundled on small logs, whose curve was too abrupt for them to roll easily up the variations between flagstone and flagstone. All eight initiates grunted at each heave on the trace-ropes, and muttered to themselves between heaves. As Pibble stood aside to allow the toiling cortège to pass him he discerned that the mutterings were the same words repeated over and over: 'The stones are my brothers. The stones are my brothers.' There was just time to repeat the formula twice between heaves. None of the six men and two women who were pulling at the ropes, nor the beldame who scuttled between back and front of the boulder setting new rollers in position, even looked at him. But at least here was a tiny mystery solved: the path to the harbour was so smooth because it had been rolled smooth.

Bruce was back at his job, now making a soft paffing noise as he broke up lumps of cement from a sack which seemed to have stood a while in the damp. Bruce hit the lumps with his mallet and some broke up into the proper fine dust, but others just became collections of grey crumbs, no more adhesive than pebbles on the beach.

'That doesn't look as if it had much strength in it,' said Pibble.

'The dust is my brother,' said Bruce, raising pious eyes.

Once again, before they could meet Pibble's, they jinked sideways, and this time Pibble understood the evasion, having seen it so often. There are more criminals than detectives in London – many more; besides, the thieves are anonymous, the thief-takers known. So Pibble was used to being recognised by apparent strangers in crowded streets, or cafeterias, or on station platforms, and the sign of recognition would be just that sideways jink of the eyes. Pibble smiled and walked on. This man, Bruce, with his El Greco visage, ought to be placeable. A common crook on this holy island, and looking more like a saint than most of the inmates. St Bruce?

No, St Bruno. So this was where he'd got to. The Yard had missed him, and the anecdotes of his legendary ambition and stupidity were growing tired. He was the one who had been persuaded by some meth-drinking scholar to forge T.S. Eliot's Fifth Quartet, *Stoke Newington*. And had almost made a killing in the Mall by offering tourists very convincing invitations to a Buckingham Palace Garden Party at ten guineas a go. And when that collection of Cape Triangular forgeries had fetched such a packet, had attempted to cash in but had spoilt his chances by producing a stamp much more like the real thing than the original forger had ever achieved. And . . . ah! He must have recognised Pibble in the Refectory, and passed the word on.

That made two of them. Rita, loopy. And Bruno, a classical numbskull. Add the stolid look of most of the green-clad brethren, and the mysterious stir in the breakfast room when Brother Servitude referred to Pibble's cleverness, and Sister Charity to the Great Dane's –

'It can't be coincidence,' he said out aloud.

The echo of the vault agreed with him just as a brown-habited Virtue swept past on some errand. Pibble couldn't remember his name – or his property, rather – but the man looked piercingly at him and said with desperate emphasis '*Twenty-eight* separate planets!' and then strode on.

So Sir Francis had made his last home on an island of idiots, and a Paradise of thieves. (Bruno wasn't the only ex-con; there was also the lock-picker.) Ah, well, it wasn't as much of a coincidence as all that: you'd need idiots if you wanted adherents who'd wear their very bones away building this crank cathedral. And like as not you'd find some of them coming out of prisons. Many criminals are rickety on their intellectual pins, and many are really only happy (if you can call it happiness) when every moment of their day is shaped by a prison-like discipline, such as the gospel of stone provided. It would be interesting to know how the original contacts were made by which the Community stocked itself with the weak in the head and the soul. And whether anybody ever got away.

Stifled with a sort of claustrophobia of the spirit, Pibble pushed open the gate into the outside world.

3

The world was all cloudscape, enormously blue and silver under the big wind. A day for kites.

Father had understood how kites worked, in theory, and had insisted that it was cheaper to make them than to buy the one in the Post Office window; but he'd never contrived one which actually flew. Pibble saw him now, in his plus-twos, fussing with a string and struts and referring to the diagram in the *BOP*, then walking confidently off while small Jamie, knees tickly with the autumn dew on the grasses, unwound the cord. Father held the contraption high and cried 'Now!' and Jamie plunged off into the wind through the cloying grey tussocks of the Common, and the cord shifted its angle as the kite rose and rose, and Father (too far off now to shout with his weak lungs) would signal to him to loose more cord the moment he turned, and the kite at once staggered, swirled, recovered for an instant as Jamie checked the run of the cord, and then dived head-long. Meanwhile the Buchan boys, smaller than Jamie and unaided by their father, had their Post Office kite steeple-high and dallying with the breeze.

Just so, now, a column of gulls dallied half a mile away to the north. There the island rose to a headland in whose crook sat a dark, plump cottage. The birds were excited; making all due allowances for anthropomorphism, Pibble could still hear that in their distant squealing. There must be something on the beach below – perhaps even a stranded whale, which the Community could trundle back into its element. Worth a visit anyhow for a copper out of *his* element and with fifty minutes to waste. He picked his way

53

along the path towards the cottage between rasping strands of heather. The heather covered about two thirds of the island, in big blotches separated by coarse grassland; from the helicopter it had looked as if a camouflage artist had painted it over.

This path also had been rolled smooth, but longer ago, judging by the fresh growth on it; as he came nearer to the cottage Pibble saw why. The grass of the headland was pocked with rectangles, like the graves of giants – there had been a village here, but all the houses were gone. Not fallen, but carefully removed, stone by stone, and rolled down the path. Only the cottage still stood.

From its door a lean collie lunged yelping the moment Pibble's bare feet chinked one granite splinter against another; but the dog was tied to the doorpost with a long cord and Pibble was able to circle out of reach. The door was propped open with a hay-rake, but no face peered out of it.

The path became rougher beyond the cottage, but more worn with use; it curled round the shoulder of the headland, then dipped to a hidden inlet. Pibble left the path and picked his way between mushroom-shaped tussocks until he reached the edge of the near cliff and could see across the inlet to the far higher cliff of the headland beyond. Against that granite wall the wind hurtled, made visible by the gulls that rode it; they dashed so fast towards the rock that he expected to see each bird end as a mess of blood and feathers there, like a moth on a windscreen, but then the upthrust wind flung them skywards to join the column; the motion was like that of those trick toys which dash for the edge of a table, feel the fall with their extra wheel and dart away. Exhilarated, Pibble stepped to the rim of his own cliff and looked over.

There was no beach in the inlet, only rocks; and no whale, only a squat, dirty fishing-boat, almost as round as a coracle. The brown sail was down but not tidied away; the part aft of the mast was open and full of a jumble of nets and rigging and oddments; on the deck in front of the mast two women sat with their backs to him, engaged in some repetitive task – ah yes, they were gutting fish and tossing the offal overboard for the gulls to scoop up and bear away. These must be the Macdonalds. They didn't wear the uniforms of the Community, but grey jerseys, tweed skirts, and brown scarves over their heads.

Pibble sat on the cliff edge for five minutes, thinking of nothing much but watching the balanced and predatory scavengers, the marching sky and the sea. The waves beyond the inlet came shoreward with a stodgy motion, breaking into fringes of white along the tops, steep-sided. They were not very big but looked uncomfortable for sailing on, and he was thankful there was a helicopter to take him to the mainland. When sitting made him cold he started back along the path.

Again the collie lunged, and again Pibble skirted round, thinking how lucky he had been to meet the affable Brother Love in the night, and not this demented guardian of bothies. His circle took him off the path at a point where the grass seemed almost downy beneath his soles; he was too early for his tryst with sinister Brother Providence, and he was also bored by the idea of going back along the same path that he'd come out by, so he decided to work his way along the cliff-tops and revisit his midnight crony.

But over the first low ridge the grassland became heather, through whose intertwined growth he began to pick his way. Each step under the billowing habit had to be a high-arched circle and then a cautious feel for the crumbly ground below. The cliff-top was a series of undulations, so that sometimes he was only a few feet above the sea-slimed boulders and sometimes leaning into the wind on a bleak ridge. The half mile to the harbour took him nearly forty minutes.

At last the heather became grassland again, a scrawny shoulder littered with boulders; from beyond it came the steady clink of hammers on stone. Pibble picked his way to the ridge expecting the grass to slope down to the cliffs above the harbour; instead he peered over a sudden drop into a huge bite that had been torn out of the hill-side – the quarry from which all those monstrous stones had been hauled to make the ugly edifice on the eastern horizon. A gang of green-clad brethren were on the floor of the quarry, chipping systematically at two big slabs that had been prized from the quarry face at a point where the granite was so fissured as to provide the beginnings of squared-up masonry. The process looked laughable, until Pibble remembered Mary's slides of Mycenean stonework, which for eighteen months she'd managed to show to almost everybody who'd set foot in the house – and still thrillingly impressive, even through the lens of a Ewell sitting room. Those palaces had been compiled by methods such as this.

At the lip of the quarry was a timber construction: the chute by which the boulders, once shaped, were lowered to the quay before being hauled on rollers up to the buildings. And, true to the Community's style, the chute was so sited that if a rock came loose in the slings it could do nothing but rocket, first bounce, into the lap of the launch. Pibble wondered whether the brown-habited engineer now bent over one of the outboard motors even looked up when the stones were slid down; or did he toil on, secure in the faith that He hath given His angels charge?

Pibble shifted to his right to examine the cause of a movement on the quay, part-hidden by the bulk of the chute. Next moment he was shouting to the stonemasons below and pointing beyond them. They looked up, and then in the direction of his gestures, but already he was running along the lip of the quarry – running so fast, with the skirts of his habit yanked up to his hips, that he almost fell headlong over the true cliff and hurtled down to the shed roof a dozen feet below. Here the quarry floor on his left was barely lower than the hillside, so he jumped down and ran for the chute. The stonemasons were staring at him, like a theatre queue at a busker – staring at Pibble and not down to the quay, where Sister Rita lay supine under the snarling jaws of Brother Love.

'Come on!' he shouted, and balanced himself on the chute. It was as steep as the pitch of a slate roof, and longer than he'd expected, but he launched himself down it in an unslowable, wallowing run.

Above the slamming of his feet on the splintery timbers he heard the clink of the stone-hammers beginning again.

He almost made it. But trying to brake a few feet from

the bottom he lost control; his legs shot forward and the side of his head hit the rim of the chute with a pain so fierce that he never noticed the ragged planks scraping at his buttocks through habit and pants. 'Go limp!' his training cried, but before his panicking limbs could obey they were sprawling out across the flagstones.

Blinded with pain and dizziness he rose to hands and knees and groped for the edge of the quay. His head felt too hurt to raise, but he willed his eyes to open and found a grey-green plain in the middle of which a crimson dome glowed. Then another glowed beside it, then a third, as the blood fell in slow drops from his nose on to the algae-mottled stone. He stood up and walked, weaving like a drunk, towards the dog and the girl.

She lay as still as a corpse but he could see the living tension in her terrified shoulders. The hound's forelegs bestrode her, its lips grinning above the reef of creamy fangs, its hackles raised like a Huron haircut. This time, groggy with his tumble and confident in last night's acquaintanceship Pibble wasn't in the least afraid.

'Good dog,' he said, in a sturdy, policemanlike voice.

At once the picture changed. The Great Dane faced round at him with a deep snarl, half-crouching for the spring. Pibble stood his ground and said, cooingly, 'Come here, boy.' The dog threw back its head and emitted a long pulsing howl. Pibble took a step nearer. The dog leaped towards him, snarling, and he backed off, arms raised to cover his face and throat. The dog, still snarling like a power saw biting into old elm, swirled back to the unmoved body of Sister Rita and stood guard again.

'Take it easy, Love sweetie,' said a plummy tenor voice.

The hackles dropped at once. The fangs vanished into amiable jowls and dewlaps. The stump of tail wagged gaily. Brother Love pranced sideways like a puppy, reared and put his forefeet on the shoulders of the brown-habited Brother who had been working at the engines of *Truth* and was now standing placidly on the quay, while the dog revelled in a thorough slobber.

When at last he fended the animal away Pibble saw that it was the helicopter pilot who had flown him over yesterday, a heavy-faced man with a film-director's crew-cut and a quick, meaningless smile. At Oban he had been affable, a little cringing, a little nervous about the unexpected passenger. Here he seemed almost childishly cocky, as though the touch of the island granite gave him power.

'You needn't have scampered like that, my old officer,' he said. 'You only got yourself all nasty and sweaty and then came a positively terrifying cropper. Love's trained to a hair, you know. He doesn't miss a trick. Not like our little Rita here. Up you get, Rita darling, and try not to come nosing round my little boat again, not without being asked.'

Sister Rita shuddered, twisted over on to hands and knees, and crawled across the quay to where Pibble stood swaying with pain and panic. Reaching him she wound her arms round his hams and laid her head softly on his hip.

'My Saviour!' she breathed.

'Take the gentleman up to Brother Patience,' said the pilot, raising his eyes in silent-film despair. 'He's got a splinter or two in his tenderest places, I'll bet.'

'Your Highness is wounded!' said Rita. She rose to her feet in anguished concern.

'Don't dilly-dally on the way, my duck,' said the pilot. 'Back you come, straight to your old Brother Tolerance. You've got a whole dice to cut, haven't you, before you can throw for a fresh square, stead of which you take it into your pretty little noddle to come nosing round my boat.'

'I'm all right,' said Pibble. 'I just got banged about a bit. But is she in a fit state . . . I mean oughtn't you . . .'

'I got salt in my upper cylinders,' said the pilot with bitchy patience. 'I know the valves are my brothers and all, but if I let 'em corrode there's a sweet lot of regrinding before they'll run again.'

'Forgive the blunt talk of our peasants,' said Rita sweetly. 'They know no better.'

Pibble started to protest again, but the pilot rounded on him, spitting slightly with the emphasis of his rage.

'And a fat lot you care for my old chopper,' he said, gesturing towards the mysterious shed. 'Oh, so I'm going to ferry you back and forth on my own wings, am I, after you come smarming over here getting me into trouble with my mates, and then not letting me alone enough to get on with my maintenance to keep her up to licensing standard? You want the rotors to flop off half way home, do you, so that you can swim the rest? That the sort of death you fancy? Well I don't!'

'Come,' sighed Rita. She offered Pibble her arm and began to lead him towards the cliff path.

'Don't you forget to come back and cut your dice, Rita,' called the pilot maliciously. 'The stones are your brothers, eh, ducky?'

'The stones are my brothers,' said Rita in her other voice and drew her arm quickly out of Pibble's, as a child shudders away from a spider in the bath. Where a small track led up to the quarry from the main path she paused.

'I must cut my dice,' she said dully. 'This time I must cut it square, and then I can begin.'

'Won't you take me to Brother Patience first?' said Pibble. '*He* said so.'

He nodded down to where the pilot was still standing watching them from the quay, one hand on the hound's magnificent brindled shoulder. The stance and habit, helped by distance, made the pair of them look like a Victorian study for a painting of St Francis.

'There are so many rules in the top of the box,' said Rita sadly. 'I can never understand them all at the same time.'

But she turned from the quarry and walked up the steep path. Pibble was oppressed by the responsibility of knowing that the pressures of the Community, however well-intentioned, were exactly calculated to increase the havoc of her mind. Her sad personality wavered like a bat down the dark crevasse between her own fantasy and Father Bountiful's.

'How long have you been on the island?' he asked.

'Time and times and the half of a time,' she said.

'How did you come?'

'Brother Servitude brought me. He found me deep in sin. I lived deliciously in Babylon, arrayed in fine linen, and the kings of the earth committed . . . committed . . . I can't remember the words . . . I'm so *hungry*.'

This was a third voice, the voice of a small girl whining

about something real. And a real voice too, neither the dismal imaginings of the Apocalypse nor the bright never-never Regency of the Children's Library bookshelf. He slowed his pace only partly because the hip that he had battered unaware in his fall had begun to ache. Hell, he thought, three days compassionate leave for urgent family reasons, and you land yourself with a loopy responsibility like this. Serve you right, Pibble, for wangling the system. Now you're going to drive poor Mary mad by wasting a fortnight's free evenings typing out an elaborate report on the Community and sending it off to all the authorities you can think of who might conceivably do something for the island's Sister Ritas – not that they will – if ever there was a haven for sleeping dogs it's Whitehall. All you'll achieve is to ruin the remnant of your career with a reputation for crankiness, while poor Rita and St Bruno and the other defenceless minds and hearts . . .

The memory of that curious flurry in the breakfast room when his own intelligence had been canvassed reminded him of the mouldy oatcake in his pocket. He fished it out and offered it to Rita. She whisked it into her own pocket with the quick snatch of a shop-lifter, then glanced round the wind-swept landscape with furtive eyes. Her left hand moved to brush back a tendril of dark hair, and in the movement a corner of oatcake slid between scarcely parted lips. Pibble gave her time to suck, rather than chew, it away before he asked his next question.

'Are you happy here?'

'I hate it. I hate it. I hate it.'

'Then why don't you leave? They can't keep you.'

'Because . . . because . . . oh, if only Your Highness knew how glad we all are to suffer for the Cause. Our lives are at your command, Sire. Weak woman that I am, I will fight to the last drop of blood in my veins for the day when your father shall come to his own again.'

'My father?'

His own inner preoccupations obliterated his irritation at her slipping gear again, and sharpened his voice with surprise, but she seemed not to notice.

'Yes, Sire. The day is coming, and coming soon, when

your royal father shall sit again upon his throne, and all shall be well with this ancient kingdom.'

Again her hand moved up to control the straying hair, conjuring a crumb into her mouth as it passed. It was astonishing how clean and glossy her locks fell over her shoulders, considering what life she was forced to live. She was beautiful too, in a way that had no special appeal to Pibble; though her hands and nails were battered with stone-masonry, and her cheeks scooped with hunger and tiredness, yet her skin was smooth and clear and her eyes sparkled as she prattled her romantic drivel. And when the wind swirled the coarse habit round her he could see that she still carried the true male-fantasy figure – taut but generous bust, embraceable waist, wide hips – dead right for the kings of the earth in Babylon. Only her features betrayed the general effect – the extraordinary smile and the longish nose, not so well shaped as to seem character-ful. Pibble could judge that even if she'd been sane she'd still have been stupid.

Judge not that ye be not judged. She was beautiful now, by the sheer vitality of youth. But a few more months – a few more weeks, even – and the discipline of the Community would set her on the bitter road to hagdom. The first thing was to get her away; nudging her towards the grammar of sanity could wait, and had better wait, for a professional.

Pibble had always disliked and distrusted amateurs, in any field. Now he looked towards the nearing spillage of buildings and wondered whether the sheer incompetence of the architecture wasn't what had first set him against the then apparently inoffensive Community. Ah well, if it was all held together with cement as poor as St Bruno had been breaking up, only the truly Cyclopean sections of masonry would stand stone on stone for long.

'My father's truest friends are across the sea,' he said.

'I know!' she cried, 'I know!'

'Was that why you were looking at the boat?'

'Yes, yes! The serf was mending it, and I wanted to be certain that it would be ready for your escape.'

'*Our* escape,' said Pibble.

61

'Your father is here!' she whispered. 'I did not know.'

'He is in hiding – he is disguised. You must have seen him often without knowing. But you must come too, um, countess. We cannot win to safety without your guidance.'

'Yours to the death!' she cried.

'Hush,' he said. 'Our enemies are very near – we must pretend again. The first thing is for you to conduct me to Brother Patience, to dress my wounds.'

She dropped at once into her sullen walk, her lips moving silently for a few seconds.

'The stones are my brothers,' she said aloud.

'Wrong voice, countess.'

She glanced at him with puzzled eyes and tried again.

'Slower,' he said, 'and duller.'

This time she managed quite a convincing imitation of her Sister Rita voice. Pibble winked to encourage her, and she flushed. Then they walked in silence under the mean gateway, the curves of whose off-Gothic arch swung up in not quite symmetrical lines, so that the masons had had to contrive an inch-wide fillet to make the keystone fit. Pibble prayed as he passed under that the join had been fixed with one of the better batches of cement.

The cloisters were loud with clacking chisels and that strange grunting mutter which accompanied the heaving of boulders. Round the first corner a group of brethren crouched down either side of a half-ton rock. Rita halted as if she and Pibble had been chattering tourists breaking into the middle of a solemn rite. Silently the whole group sank to their knees and placed their hands palm downwards on the boulder. Looking along the unfinished corridor to his left, Pibble could see the gap into which the stone would fit, about three feet above the level of the paving. All together, without any apparent signal, they broke into a low chant, so drilled that every word was clear: 'And it shall be on the day when ye pass over Jordan unto the land which the Lord giveth thee, that thou shalt set thee up great stones.' A few seconds' silence and they rose in a brisk flurry, like pigeons from a wheatfield.

The little man at the head of the stone looked along the corridor and scratched his jaw. 'Question is,' he said, 'do we take her along on the rollers or do we tip her up and walk her along?'

'Fair old distance to walk her,' said one of the others.

'But we got the space to tip her here, see?' said the little man.

'I reckon we could tip her there,' said the second man. 'After all, we did it with a dice this big in the passage to the lonely cells.'

'Right you are,' said the little man, 'but we didn't have to set that 'un in so high, not half.'

'Look,' said the second man. 'We roll her along, set a step for her a bit beyond, tip her on to that, set a step back this way, and I reckon we could get her up in three.'

'We've got something to lash her to down there,' said the little man.

'Rope's been rubbing something dreadful,' said a third.

'No use grumbling about that,' said the little man. 'You heard Brother Courage say as there wasn't no more.'

Rita was plucking at Pibble's sleeve, and he allowed himself to be led on, wincing now as he walked; but for his soreness he'd have liked to stay and see how the alliance of muscle and prayer coped with the formidable and risky manoeuvre of setting the huge stone into place. Brother Providence was walking along the cloisters towards them when they came round the next corner.

'I'm afraid I'm late,' said Pibble. 'I had a bit of a fall.'

'Five minutes only, Superintendent. We have all learned to wait, we who are sealed.'

Brother Providence spoke with donnish calm, but was watching Rita, not Pibble, and with a hot, unwinking stare. She stood her ground but Pibble thought he could sense an inward cringing, like that of a hound so used to beating that it interprets any movement as a coming blow.

'The brother down at the harbour, the pilot, asked Sister Rita to bring me up,' he said. 'He told her to take me to see Brother Patience.'

'Yes, yes,' said Brother Providence in a preoccupied way. 'Bad as that, was it? tsk tsk. I'll take you myself. Now, Rita, back you go to the cup and finish cutting your dice, and may the Great Mason strengthen your wrist and

63

straighten your eye.'

She bowed her head, turned and walked away. Only when she had vanished round the corner pillar did Brother Providence withdraw his stare from the sad, slim figure. Nasty old man, thought Pibble automatically – but no, it was not the gaze which follows the jigging hams of typists. It was Frank Truelove's look. Frank was a colleague of Pibble's, a hard-working and dedicated copper, with a special knack of persuading statements out of tight-lipped villains, especially young ones. Pibble had seen Frank with exactly that stare on his face in the lull of a long interrogation. Twice, he knew, Frank had only escaped sacking by the fluke of his victims' being part of cases too big to lose for the sake of one near-psychotic bobby.

'I tried to come down the chute from the quarry,' he said. 'But I lost my balance.'

'*Durus descensus Averno*,' said Brother Providence, using the Old Pronunciation. 'And you found our Cerberus at the bottom, I dare say.'

'Yes,' said Pibble, 'Brother Love was there.'

Whatever current Brother Providence had switched on for Rita, he had forgotten to switch off for Pibble, who had to drop his gaze to avoid the direct challenge of the yellow eyes. Yes, certainly the lust that fired them was far from drooling; no erosion of years would bring it to impotence; with such a glance do scheming patriarchs remodel codicils in their wheel-chairs, for the last pleasure of watching their heirs skip and submit.

'It won't take Brother Patience five minutes to patch me up,' he said. 'Then perhaps you'd be kind enough to take me round and explain the work of the Community. I really am most interested. I've never come across an organisation like this before.'

'Good, good,' said Brother Providence. 'Patience keeps a useful little surgery. This way. We don't make much use of it ourselves. One of the first ladders we climb on the board takes us past the ailments of the flesh. He is more concerned with balancing our diet.'

He led Pibble along that side of the cloister, past the steps up to Sir Francis's rooms and the niche where Brother

64

Hope had endured his electronic vigil, round the corner and all down the blank wall of the Refectory. Straight ahead lay a finished passage, parallel to the one off which Pibble's own cell opened. Pibble was still dazed with the irony of owing an insight to Frank Truelove, but a corner of his mind was also teased by an architectural anomaly as Brother Providence led him up this passage: there were doors on both sides of it, but those on the right couldn't lead to anything larger than a cupboard, or if they led into cells the cells would be windowless. His own passage, which had doors only along the far side, ran too close for anything else.

'Patience,' said Brother Providence, throwing open the furthest door without knocking, 'you have a chance to prove whether your hand has lost the cunning it had in Babylon. Our guest has taken a nasty tumble.'

Brother Patience rose from behind a rough table on which he had been working at some finicky task. Pibble recognised the box of chalks he had nursed in the helicopter. He also recognised the doctor-monk from breakfast, where he had stood out by being markedly the oldest of the Virtues – unless the scooped and wrinkled cheeks meant that the man had endured at some time a withering sickness or disease.

'Dear me,' he said. 'Take your habit off and we'll see what we can do for you.'

His voice was almost toneless with huskiness, like that of a true chain-smoker, though Pibble doubted if there was as much as a single fag on the island – even supposing the Community *were* peopled with old lags, he couldn't see any of them being allowed to set up as tobacco barons.

'I'll take a turn or two round the cloisters,' said Brother Providence pleasantly, and left. Pibble stripped off his habit.

'I banged the side of my head,' he said. And my nose bled a bit. And I've done something to this hip. And I must have scraped my arse without noticing, because that's hurting worse than anything now.'

'Dear me,' said Brother Patience without solicitude. 'When did you last have a tetanus jab, do you know?'

'Last April.'

'Well, that's all right. I shall work from the top down. Perhaps you've cracked your skull, but that's not as serious as it sounds, old chap. How old are you, in fact?'

'Fifty-four.'

'Hm. Your condition's not bad, for Babylon. Tell me if I hurt you more than if it were normal bruising. You'll know the difference.'

His hands moved through Pibble's hair, strong and confident, but trembling all the time.

'Can't tell without an X-ray,' he said at last. 'Your ear's never going to be as handsome as it used to be, and we'll just have to pray that the bone's in good nick.'

With a curious prickle of dread Pibble realised that he meant the verb literally. The painful struggle out of his vest seemed a good moment to step on to quaggy ground.

'Sister Rita's a schizophrenic, isn't she?'

'That's the normal jargon,' said Brother Patience after a short pause.

'Shouldn't she be having treatment – I mean more elaborate treatment than you can manage here?'

'Does that hurt?'

'Yes, but only on the surface. Shouldn't she?'

'You've caught yourself a nasty wallop, but your ribs seem sound and the contusions indicate that the blow missed your femur, though you may have chipped the top edge.'

'Do you think, as a doctor, that the pressures of the Community are, well, the right thing for her?'

Brother Patience sighed and straightened up.

'When I was a doctor,' he said, 'I might have agreed with you. Now that I am sealed and have moved many squares from Babylon I know that I would have been wrong. The City we are building is the answer to every patient's need, however sick he may be in spirit or mind or flesh. From Providence to Love we are all being treated, all being trained. Take your pants down. No clinic in Babylon, however sympathetic, could give Rita the treatment she receives here, because no clinic in Babylon could truly understand the nature of her illness. Great Scott, you've done yourself an injury there, old chap. I'll take those splinters out if I can find my tweezers – here we are – this is going to hurt. It is her immortal soul which is being cured, and not just the feeble mind and perishable flesh. Stand still, man. Flesh, bone, brain, nerve, id, ego, superego, that's all nonsense. It'll have to be iodine, as I don't stock anything else. It doesn't really matter what happens to them, as the only reality is the soul. This will hurt too.'

'But wouldn't her soul stand a better chance if the rest of her were allowed to come to terms with itself first? You seem to me to be trying her fearfully hard. Ouch.'

'I told you it would hurt. You mustn't think, old man, that we haven't considered that point, in fact I've said much the same thing to Providence myself. He shot me down. No splinters this side, but it's pretty raw. Grit your teeth, old man. Great Scott, what was that noise?'

Pibble never heard the noise. At one moment he was warming towards this struck-off medico for having refrained from the joke about turning the other cheek. At the next he was weeping with remembered pain renewed.

Father would never have beaten a child, even his own; but Ted Fasting had once caught small Jamie standing in the onion bed to reach for a copy-book which Sam had tossed over the fence for a lark. Fat, waistcoated Mr Fasting, his big face blue with insult, had larruped Jamie with a bunch of pea-sticks, holding the wriggling neck down with one greasy hand and thrashing with the other, until the blood came. Just so did the iodine bite in. In the fog of his tears Pibble could see the neat hem of turf round the sieved soil of the onion-bed; the huge, striped, brown-glistening bulbs; and the green haulms spearing upwards.

'That should do,' said Brother Patience. 'You'll be eating off the mantelpiece for a week or so.'

Pibble straightened and shook his head to clear the fog from his eyes. Mother had wanted to send for the Cruelty Man, but Father had strolled down the street that evening to have a chat with Mr Fasting. Thereafter a strange coolness had existed between the two families, long-lasting, quite different from the ten-day, quickly forgotten feuds which always racked the street. It was years since Pibble had thought of that beating or its aftermath, but now he realised that Father's chat had certainly been an attempt to explain to Mr Fasting the nature of the inner drives that made him so ready to thrash the stretched buttocks of small boys.

'Please,' said a voice from the door. Pibble recognised the lean, green-habited man who stood there; he came from the stone-shifting gang and had complained about the wear on the rope. Now his eyes shone with the first real pleasure and excitement that Pibble had seen on any countenance since he'd stepped out of the helicopter – unless you counted the doggy ecstasy in Brother Love's starlit eyes.

'Yes,' said Brother Patience in the universal tone of doctors interrupted at their job. Pibble tenderly pulled up his pants.

'Brother Providence says to come, please,' said the man. 'The rope busted and we dropped a whopping dice on Gav's ankle. You should have heard him holler.'

'We did,' said Brother Patience calmly, and strode out. Pibble edged into his vest, but before he had his habit on the doctor was back to pick up the big octagonal bottle of iodine and four or five old bandages out of a drawer. Nothing to allay pain, Pibble noticed; no morphia, not even any aspirin; only the agonising disinfectant.

Dressed, Pibble mooned about. The surgery was as poorly equipped as any witch-doctor's: two clinical thermometers in a dusty jug; a stethoscope; a sweet-jar full of senna-pods; a bottle of white pills labelled cortisone, such as Sir Francis had frowned over at breakfast; volume one of a dictionary of diseases. Beside the carton of chalks on the table was a pestle and mortar with a little white powder in the bottom; two mixing bowls, one clean and one containing the yolk of an egg with the hard scum of exposure to air on it; an egg-shell; a lozenge tin containing six more white pills; and a curious bit of soldered metal, like a doll's baking-tin, in which the doll could have baked eight tea-cakes the size of a pill.

Pibble stared at the collection, humming, forgetting his pains. Um. Order school chalk from the mainland, grind it up; mix it with white of egg; bake eight pills overnight; give the old man two; that leaves six; put them in a lozenge-tin. Pibble hunted through drawers and found nothing that could conceivably be poison. So there ought to be a couple of days to play with, surely.

Best not be found in too Nosey-Parkerish an occupation. He put everything back as near as possible where it had been and picked up the only reading matter in the room.

A naked, moon-faced mulatto was the subject of the drab photograph on the page where the book opened; he was posed sideways to show the characteristic striations on the hips – some adrenal deficiency, according to the text. The next entry woke the unreliable goblin who presided over Pibble's memory. Who would not weep if Addison were he, said the goblin. The bartons' lodger had had Addison's disease, a malfunction of the adrenal gland. The salt was part of his treatment.

And that was where the book had chosen to open. Pibble flipped through the other pages and found that the glossy-coated leaves moved as if they had seldom been separated; but these few pages towards the end of the book were soft with much turning. He read rapidly, keyed for the pad of returning soles. Lethargy, sudden falling asleep, character-istic pigmentation of the skin, treatment with cortisone and hydrocortisone, twice daily, elderly to be given cortisone only with salt instead of the hydrocortisone, danger from secondary infections, first symptoms often manifested after physical shock especially surgery, lapse in treatment likely to lead to rapid collapse and irreversible brain-damage.

Sir Francis was pink, not brown, but perhaps the corti-sone had kept him so. And there was nothing in the text about the lethargy coming at precisely regular intervals, nor not sleeping for twenty-seven years, but the rest fitted as pat as the final piece of a jigsaw. The white pill was cortisone, the salt, because he was elderly. He'd had an operation, maybe to cope with incontinence, witness Rutherford's rug and his damned bladder. Nor could the old man send for someone and tell him to take the mike away – things a'n't like that, not like that at all. Kick too much for the comfort of the Community, and where's your cortisone? Twenty-four hours would crumble the most famous intellect in Europe into a senile shambles.

For a few clear-headed seconds Pibble knew which side he was on. Hitherto Pibble had been neutral between his two hereditary enemies, the betrayer of his father and the seducers of his mother. (Mr Toger could not be present, so the whole Community stood proxy.) But murder is murder.

The dust-mark on the shelf showed where the book had lain, so he put it carefully back. The bottle had about a dozen of the genuine white pills left in it, and Pibble considered swapping six of them for the fake ones in the lozenge-tin; but they were so obviously more professional that it was too much of a risk – Patience would be sure to pick among them to choose the least deficient, and then to spot that they were all suddenly perfect. No one is so aware of the blemishes in his work as the actual forger.

Instead he took two pills out of the bottle and knotted them into the corner of his handkerchief. He would like to have taken more, but three seemed to diminish the contents by a noticeable amount.

4

Well, then, the only other natural way to be found waiting was staring out of the window. The line where sea met sky was quite clear under the scouring wind, which hissed round an ill-fitting pane like a groom rubbing a horse down – the draggled pony that had pulled the Clapham Patent Bread Company van and had been stabled behind the Pakenham Arms, where old Simon the pot-boy had inexpertly tended the poor beast in preparation for the dream time coming when he'd go and live in the country and have a little farm of his own. Hinges creaked.

'Ready?' said Brother Providence's donnish voice.

'I hope nobody was badly hurt,' said Pibble.

'Hurt?'

'I thought a stone had fallen on someone's ankle – Gavin's.'

'Alas, Superintendent, one forgets how to think in these terms. God has chosen to punish us by breaking the leg of a strong workman. Compared with the shock of that the hurt is nothing, an illusion of fallen matter.'

And the iodine was nothing. And Ted Fasting's peasticks nothing.

'Do many of these, um, punishments happen?' said Pibble.

'None hitherto.'

'I hope it isn't me that brought you the bad luck,' said Pibble. The presence of the bearded monk seemed to bring inanities to his lips unwilled. And the remark was a mistake, too – not for its inanity but for some other unguessable reason. Brother Providence's remote amber gaze

71

became intent as a lepidopterist's, and his tone darkened.

'Luck is an illusion also,' he said. 'Nothing occurs without reason. We will begin by climbing the tower.'

Sister Dorothy came striding along the cloisters towards them, grim-faced, carrying a steaming enamel jug. Pibble, used to the lightning instincts of London pavements, veered a little to his left to let her pass, expecting her to do the same; but she came on like an ironclad, seemed only to see him when she was a foot or two away, started to say something but stopped as she plunged into him, tilting a gill of hot water over his thigh. Swearing under her breath she staggered towards a pillar, hugged it with her free arm, waited for the jug to stop slopping, and marched off without even a snort of apology. Behind her the chill air reeked like a Dublin pub.

'Sister Dorothy seems an unusual member of the Community,' suggested Pibble.

'She was tight,' said Brother Providence calmly.

'I had not imagined that you made use of spirits,' said Pibble. The prim phrase and the primmer tone were Mr Toger's, remembered from a doorstep conversation when Mr Toger, an Elder of the vehemently teetotal sect to which Mother belonged, had called one evening after Mother had taken a dose or two of her 'medicine'. Early 'thirties, maybe.

'. . . no alcohol anywhere on the island,' he heard Brother Providence saying with exactly the same calm. A faith whose founder converses with intelligent cuttlefish could presumably resolve this mundane contradiction; it didn't make for easy conversation.

The tower door was the one directly opposite the entrance to Sir Francis's rooms. While Brother Providence fished for the key in the green corduroys which he wore under his habit, Pibble glanced to where the flex of the microphone had lain. It was gone.

'This is the first locked door I've seen on the island,' said Pibble.

'In the Faith of the Sealed, stairs have a special significance. One does not want any of the simpler brethren confusing this sinful stone with the spiritual reality.'

72

'But I thought stone was, er, OK for you.'

'Sinful stone, Superintendent, sinful flesh. Both are made of sinful atoms. We cannot, in our fallen nature, carve our spirits to the perfect squares needed to compose the Great Board, but we can practise the necessary discipline on stone. It is not for nothing that the right-angle is so called, but it needs discipline to achieve it.'

'Ouch!' cried Pibble, bashing his bruised toe into a particularly ill-disciplined riser in the dark stairwell.

'The stones are your brothers,' said Brother Providence.

'Do you mean that the City you are actually building here is really only a sort of metaphor?' said Pibble.

His guide sighed, turned and sat down on a stair. Pibble, conscious of the condition of his buttocks, leaned against the outer wall. Brother Providence had chosen a spot where a slit window let in a patch of grey north light in such a way that his face and beard showed clear but all the rest of him was a formless presence in the dimness. The head seemed to float unbodied, and as it talked the curl of the stair gave the careful vowels a chill resonance, as of dungeons.

'You are using terrible words in a loose and frivolous fashion, Superintendent. I tremble for your immortal soul. The first thing to understand is that there are degrees of reality. The central reality is God, and all religions and faiths are instinctive attempts to arrive at that reality, but in our fallen nature the faiths have hitherto been mistaken, often leading their believers still deeper into illusion. The next degree of reality is the soul's relationship with God. The sacrifice of God is a broken spirit. That is the one truth above all others. A broken spirit is a spirit which has been reduced to its constituent elements so that it can be remoulded into a shape wherein it can come to its God freed from all the shackles of fallen matter. The third degree of reality is the method by which this remoulding can be achieved, and the only method, we now know, is the Faith of the Sealed. The City is part of this Faith. From the higher degrees, the Faith may indeed be, in your word, no more than a metaphor; but from the innumerable degrees below it is a very powerful reality.'

The man was a hypnotist. Only Pibble's arches, prodding him with their own realities, kept him from surrender.

'You mean your faith is a tool for breaking people's spirits,' he said.

'That is a way of putting it. You must remember that a tool, to be useful, must be strongly held. And so must a faith. A powerful mind must grasp it before it can be properly used.'

'Aren't analogies dangerous too?'

(Interrupt, and perhaps the spell will weave itself into a tangle.)

'Most are indeed barren, Superintendent. But some were sown into the language, built into the very shape of the human mind, as clues to lead us to our true destiny. You will have noticed, for instance, that we speak frequently of the relationship of brotherhood. This is to remind us that we must, in the words of the poet, die of the absolute paternal care . . .'

'My father wasn't like that at all,' said Pibble, with bright interest, tangling the web again. Brother Providence rose with another sigh and started to climb the stairs. Pibble followed, wondering whether his slight grogginess came from delayed shock at his fall or from the sense of having beaten off a sudden, violent ambush. Crippen, this was a nasty creed. Or perhaps it was only nastily explicit. Even at fifteen, shambling up the street with his torn satchel under his arm, Jamie had sensed that Mr Toger would have liked to have come a good deal further into the house than the doorstep, and comforted the smooth-skinned widow with more than tracts.

Where had Providence come from, Pibble wondered. What had he been in Babylon? There was something teasing about his manner of speech. Donnish, he'd first decided, but now he felt that was wrong; there was a man-of-affairs undertone too, and a sort of social ease that hinted at a life among the nobs. Also, unconnected with this, a curious feeling that he knew Pibble better than Pibble knew him. It made Pibble uncomfortable.

At the top of the stairs Providence lifted a trap-door to let in the brimming light and the hissing, gull-riddled air.

'What a marvellous view,' said Pibble.

'All the kingdoms of the earth.'

'Really?'

'Really in our terms, metaphorically in yours.' No ambush here – the smile was that of any New Theologian expounding on *Meeting Point* a paradox which he knows his four million viewers are too crass to resolve.

'I'm not so sure of my own terms as you are of yours,' said Pibble.

'Tell me why you came here, Superintendent. I know that Simplicity contrived to invite you – without telling us, I may say – but it must have been inconvenient for a busy policeman, and I am sure you are not the type to make a tedious journey for the pleasure of meeting a famous name.'

'It's difficult to explain,' said Pibble. 'I was an only child and my father died when I was eleven. He mattered a lot to me, and I've always wanted to know more about him – in a rather obsessive way, you might say. Anyway, he worked for Sir Francis for several years before the First World War, and when Sir Francis sent for me I thought it would be my last chance of meeting anyone who knew him in that period. The letter reached me in a roundabout way, and he'd given me a final date which was to-day, so I had to come in a hurry.'

'Why should he do that?'

'I think he thought the letter mightn't reach me, and he wanted to feel that there was a date beyond which he wouldn't expect me any longer.'

'It seems a curious way to acquire information for his book. He cannot have expected you to have much to contribute.'

'I thought the book was supposed to be some sort of a secret.'

Brother Providence laughed benignly.

'My dear man,' he said, 'how can it be a secret? I should think the sections he has finished must be being translated into forty languages at this very moment. Why, it's my only regret since I left Babylon that I shall never be able to read it.'

'I meant a secret among the Community.'

'Strange.'

'Well, nobody talked about it, and otherwise I'd have thought they would have. It must be quite an excitement for you all.'

'Our excitements are not of this world, Superintendent.'

'I meant that having publishers and editors coming and going must have been a bit of a disruption.'

'Simplicity conducted all his negotiations by post. The first we knew of the book was the arrival of two journalists in a launch, wishing to interview him. That would have been about five weeks ago, but we told them how ill he was and they left. I believe he made it a condition of his contract that he was not to be disturbed by visitors from the journals which are printing the extracts.'

'How ill is he?'

Brother Providence smiled sweetly as the wind fidgeted with his beard and slapped the straining folds of his habit against his legs.

'Ah, Superintendent,' he said, 'you have caught us out. We were guilty of some exaggeration in our negotiations with the press-men. Answer a fool according to his folly, eh?'

'My wife showed me a rumour in her paper about his being sick,' said Pibble. 'By the way, how did you know I was a policeman?'

'Some of the Sealed are ex-criminals, and it happened that one of them had actually been through your hands, and recognised you. I doubt if you would recognise *him*, now.'

And that was a joke, a confident if secret teasing. You could hear it in his voice, though the beard hid any smile. And, hell, it might all be true, and only Sir Francis lying – a man who has betrayed one Pibble (so Mother always maintained) could now betray another. Pibble only just prevented his hand from straying to his pocket to feel if the two pills were real and there; instead he peered round at the mottled and monotonous landscape, the blank and monotonous sea. The Isle of Tiree brooded on the northern horizon; Scotland lay east, but the driven clouds had massed against the land and it wasn't visible. To the south-

76

east Dubh Artach light house notched the horizon, but apart from that the visible world was bleakly mediaeval.

'I suppose you keep the helicopter in the shed on the quay,' he said, 'so that the dog can guard the boat as well.'

'Yes, Love is enough – William Morris, I think?'

(Now, *who* would draw attention to his little crossword-clue joke in exactly that accent?)

'You seem to have some very modern equipment for a . . . well . . .'

'A society so deliberately Spartan, you wish to say? Say it, my dear man – we have no feelings to hurt. But we need the boat, the helicopter and the radio for communications with the mainland. Would that we needed none, until it pleases the Lord to send us more success with our crops; the authorities on the mainland insist on the radio.'

'And I suppose you have a generator to provide Sir Francis with electric light.'

'And for the radio also, but for nothing else.'

(Slight over-emphasis there. What else might they need a generator for?)

'Shall we go down now?' said Brother Providence. 'I see you are not wearing trousers, so you will find it cold in this wind.'

'You too,' said Pibble.

'The wind bloweth whither it listeth, and is nothing to us, only fallen matter at its most irrational.'

'Brother Hope has a remarkable physique. I saw him in contemplation last night.'

'So he told me. I'm sorry to say that you interrupted at an exciting moment. After Father Bountiful, Hope was the first of all the Sealed. He alone, so far, has achieved anything like Father Bountiful's powers of soul-transfer. This is a central technique in the Faith of the Sealed, as it enables us to search for peoples who have progressed further along the path of regeneration than poor, fallen man. Last night Hope was achieving, for the first time, contact with the souls of another sphere, and you brought him back. Did you hear anything?'

'It sounded like voices,' said Pibble.

'Very likely. They wouldn't, of course, be voices from

77

another planet. The technique is in some ways like a strong spiritual current, which sets up eddies round it, displacing local phenomena in curious ways. When Father Bountiful was among us, we became accustomed to hearing snatches of conversation from adjoining rooms.'

'I've no experience of this sort of thing,' said Pibble doubtfully. 'I'm sorry if I interrupted.'

'The interruption was willed by the Lord,' said the monk, stepping into the dark stairway, 'and Gavin's ankle was broken to confirm His will. We are not yet worthy. Be careful – the seventh stair is the sinful one.'

Um, thought Pibble, ingenious, given their premises. Could they really think he believed it? This bullying intelligence on the stairs below him couldn't be that naïve – or did he have pockets of naïvety, geodes in the flinty mind? No, more likely they'd think he thought they thought he believed them – but that meant they didn't mind his knowing they knew he knew about the microphone. Dizzy with this double helix of deception and the single helix of the stairs he padded out into the cloisters. They were trying to kill the old man – hold fast to that.

The rest of the tour was boring. The buildings held nothing but a succession of small rooms, meanly proportioned. The Refectory, which occupied almost the whole length of the cloisters on the side to the left of the tower, was more nobly conceived but had come out not a whit less ugly. The Virtues slept in cells which guarded the harsh dormitories of the green-robed initiates. Presumably Rita had slipped past her warders when they too were worn down with the long abrasions of the day and deep in the ozonised sleep of the sea-wind.

The day was certainly hard. Pibble was shown a large patch to the east of the buildings where stunted broccoli leaned from the wind like thorn trees on the Downs; beyond, a scum of green on the sour earth showed where the spring oats were coming up; beyond that a gang of the brethren were subduing a new stretch of soil. But most of the inmates were involved in the ceaseless expansion of the buildings themselves, digging the foundations for a second square of cloisters, or adding a storey to one side of the existing ones. They climbed a warped ladder to see how this was done.

The process was curious, and in its way ingenious. The Refectory was two storeys high already, but beyond it three sets of vaulted ground-floor cells ran westwards – first the set with the doctor's room at the end, then the puzzling line of windowless cells, and finally the guest cells. The storey over the first vault was now almost finished and was being roofed with the rafters and slates from the second vault, whose long hummock of rough grey stone now lay exposed and ready for its own second storey, which in turn would be topped off with the roof from the guest-cells. It was a kind of masonic leap-frog.

Brother Providence pointed and explained. The gangs of initiates hauled, heaved and cemented, silent except for the rapid patter of prayer whenever any large stone had to be cajoled into place. St Bruno had vanished, and another man was doing his job. The gulls creaked, the wind hissed, the far foam snored, and the easy voice beside Pibble spoke of discipline. No, they did not labour at the stones all day; after dinner they resorted to more spiritual disciplines, most of the brethren learning the art of meditation in the Refectory, unless called out to join special groups for exercises of the soul under the guidance of one Virtue. Those in particular need, such as poor Rita, received individual help in the difficult disciplines of world-renunciation – Providence himself was called to give that help, while Brother Hope was specially adept in the management of small groups. In the winter, of course, when the days were so short in these latitudes, all worked on the stones while it was light and did their spiritual exercises in the dark. The dark, indeed, could be a great help to certain stubborn souls; if only it were possible to still all the fallen senses at once, then the path of renunciation would be markedly smoother. No, Brother Simplicity no longer joined them in these disciplines, and neither did Sister Dorothy. They had never been sealed, but when Simplicity had made his final throw and gone to the ultimate squares, no doubt Sister

Dorothy would join them with a whole heart.

'She'll be a tough nut,' said Pibble, unthinkingly.

Brother Providence appeared not to notice this hint that the methods of the Community were no more than routine will-breaking, such as innumerable faiths have seen, feeding innumerable inquisitions, filling innumerable prisons. The thought of prisons chimed with a gang of initiates trooping back from some task of stone-displacement in shuffling silence at a pace he had seen before, the dreary step of convicts to and from the exercise yard or their day's work. Remembering Providence's mysterious challenge he scanned the group for familiar faces; one woke a faint echo. There ought, by rights, to be a third-rate lock-picker somewhere about – perhaps the very man who'd recognised Pibble. St Bruno would have made more mess of the lock than that faint curl of swarf – where *was* St Bruno? And another thing, what had brought the several ex-cons whom the monk had spoken of to this unlikely preventive detention?

He was aware of a sharpness, a pay-attention-boy note, in Brother Providence's last remark. (Got it! The man had been a schoolmaster!)

'I'm sorry,' he said. 'There's so much to take in at one go – the mind becomes numbed.'

'Ah.'

The big head nodded understandingly. If you took St Bruno, or Rita, as your yardstick numb minds were the Community's stock-in-trade.

'Did you ask me something?' said Pibble.

'No matter, my dear fellow. It must seem a contrast to the routine of your normal life. I too have known routines.'

The problem of the trout which wishes to retain the angler's interest is to nose at the fly without disdain.

'Yes,' said Pibble, 'it's a contrast all right. I don't know quite what to make of it yet. It certainly has its . . . um . . . '

'Attraction? Yes, even a child can be attracted by the shape and colour of the board. There is hope, and more than hope, for all these –' he nodded towards a trudging gang – 'because they have with our help become as little children.'

'I know you'll think it's none of my business,' said Pibble, 'but I'm worried about Sister Rita. I'd have thought a psychiatrist –'

'You are talking the language of Babylon,' said the monk sharply. 'There is a Babylon of the mind as well as of the body. In the Babylon of the body sister Rita was a harlot, though she came from quite a good family – distant connections of the Howards, to use the language of Babylon for a moment. She was at a dozen schools, then ran away with a group of popular musicians who introduced her to drugs before deserting her. She was found by Servitude supporting herself in Paddington under the guise of Senorita Rita, Spanish Exercises. The drugs, of course, are responsible for her mental state. Drugs. Matter which enslaves mind. The epitome of Babylon. I have been in touch with her family, and they are relieved to know that she is in our care. Our discipline is certainly hard for such a creature, deliberately hard, but we make sure that it is not hard beyond her endurance. And what we give her is not the palliatives of your Babylonish psychiatrists. They, even when successful in their own terms, merely make a soul content with whatever happens to be its state in the mess of fallen matter. We *cure*.'

'How did Brother Servitude come across her?'

'We are not as enclosed a Community as you may think, Superintendent. For instance, under the laws of Babylon we are a charity, and this demands negotiations with the tax people and other authorities. I myself have been to London twice this winter. Servitude goes more often. The Eternal City will need a great army of masons, and their recruitment is Servitude's particular care. He has always been a seeker, sifting the faiths of Babylon until the Lord guided him to the true one, and he has many acquaintances among the priests of those faiths. I think someone in the Salvation Army introduced him to Rita.'

Yes, Servitude, the garrulous gunner, was a lost-ten-tribesman, if ever. Useful to know that Providence had been in London, though the theft of the manuscript would have to wait. Pibble had deliberately asked no more about it than was plausible, and was already regretting having put

81

his guide's back up by trying to do his duty by Rita. She would have to wait too. Time to shift the talk to a less touchy area.

'You draw your members from a fascinatingly wide range,' he said. 'I was wondering about your pilot's past history.'

But the monk reacted as though Pibble had once more stepped on to ground where trespassers are shown coldly out by a gamekeeper with a gun under his arm.

'I suppose there's no harm your knowing,' he said after a pause. 'Tolerance was a garage hand who had the misfortune to win a talent contest on television and decided to try his luck as a professional performer; but, as I have told you, luck is an illusion – he was willed towards the stage and then spared the hideous tortures of fame, and so willed for a while into ill company, and all for the single purpose of Brother Servitude finding him and bringing him to work for the City. Now I believe I have shown you all there is to see, though only a crumb of all there is to know. What would you prefer to do next?'

Pibble looked at his watch. Just after eleven.

'I think Sir Francis should be ready to see me quite soon,' he said. 'Are you sure it's all right for me to stay for another day or two? If . . .'

'As a matter of fact it would suit us much better if you stayed. Tolerance has some mechanical work to do to both *Truth* and the helicopter, and if he stays at the harbour he can keep watch on Rita while she re-cuts her die. If he flies you back, we shall have to spare another Virtue from the afternoon's exercises.'

'Doesn't she do them?'

'No. The full Refectory confuses her mind, filling it with imaginings of the courts of the Kings of Babylon. She is one who must be guided alone.'

'Oh,' said Pibble. 'Shall I come and see you when I've finished with Sir Francis?'

'Please do. Come to my office. If we were back in Babylon I should have been able to offer you Madeira before luncheon.'

'I'm grateful enough anyway. This has been a most

thought-provoking experience.'

'I hope so,' said Brother Providence casually, and strode off along the cloisters.

Pibble walked more slowly the other way. Madeira before luncheon. Distant *connections* of the Howards. A very posh brand of schoolmaster indeed, Brother Providence must have been. Unnerving – both in the elemental power of personality which he seemed able to call out at will, in the way that a snake-charmer conjures the cold beast out of a basket; and also in the deliberate, unsweating, willed social expertise, which all the world's Pibbles long for, are ashamed of their longing, and know they will never achieve. And then this terrifying faith, with its garnishing of biblical cress – and the man believed in it, and believed that he was doing his victims *good*. Awful, hideous – or was Pibble's revulsion and distrust a legacy from Mr Toger? His own faith was a disorderly drawerful of doubts, but at least it included a doubt of his own motives. Was it possible that the emotional stimulus of meeting Sir Francis at last, and summoning Father out of limbo, had also summoned other wraiths, a dismal chorus of Mother's dour friends? Could he have been hating and distrusting the Community for revenge – stale, mean revenge?

Come, Pibble, there was the microphone. But that could be explained. There were the fake pills, and perhaps they could too. A doctor must be entitled to administer placebos, though the book said . . . There was the picked lock. And Sir Francis, known traitor, might have done that in the course of some unfathomable deception. There was Rita, whose family approved of her presence here. Yes, she was morally inescapable, but not evidence.

Hope was at his niche, not meditating but leaning casually against the wall, arms folded and legs crossed, watching the bustle of work as an office messenger watches the cranes on a building site. This time the flex snaked upwards, an eerie echo of the cold beast out of the basket. Pibble shivered, nodded, and climbed the stairs.

Sister Dorothy was also leaning against a wall in an attitude which showed she couldn't have stood without its help. She prodded an envelope towards Pibble as he came up.

'Prov says to give him this,' she said in a thick whisper. 'Don't want the old sod to see me. Christ, I feel bloody queer.'

'Why don't you sit down for a bit?' said Pibble.

He had to catch her as she slumped on to the top step. She groaned and hid her face in her hands. Pibble eased her against the wall again and went into the room.

Sir Francis was sitting in his chair, but not as before. Now he looked truly old. The shoulders were stooped, the eyes lacked their fire. But the voice didn't.

'You're two minutes late, you damned idiot. My time's precious – yours isn't.'

As he spoke he pointed over Pibble's shoulder towards the vault.

'I'm terribly sorry,' said Pibble and wheeled round.

There hung the microphone, ten feet from the floor, plain to see once you'd looked for it but unreachable except with a ladder. Its flex left through a small hole in the vault, made by bashing out a fillet of stone. A few chips of rubble still lay on the carpet.

'That's what your damned fool of a father was always saying,' said Sir Francis, pushing a small pad of paper at Pibble.

'I've remembered quite a bit more about him,' said Pibble as he took it. The writing seemed as firm as ever – or was there a flicker in the spiky loops? It said 'My pill was different this morning. Wrong texture. Get me out or get a proper doctor here. Use your authority. Twelve hours'. Presumably the rest of the message had been interrupted by Pibble's arrival. He fished in the pouch of his habit for his handkerchief, unknotted it and let the white tablets fall into his palm. He handed them to the old man.

'Clever of you,' snarled Sir Francis. 'Damned unmemorable fellow if ever I met one.'

He took the tablets, tried one on his tongue, nodded, picked up a glass of water from the table by his chair and washed it down. The other he slipped into the back of his fob watch.

'The trouble is,' said Pibble, 'that all the things I remember are little unconnected bits, the way a child does

84

remember things. Perhaps if you were to tell me your end, then I'd be able to piece together a more coherent pattern for you.'

'Not on your damned life,' said Sir Francis. 'That's my job, piecing patterns together. Always has been.'

'It's mine, too.'

'Tchah! Call the random buffoonery of prisoners a *pattern*? You tell me. Sit down.'

'I can't,' said Pibble. 'I had a fall and hurt my arse.'

Sir Francis cackled with real pleasure. Pibble jerked his thumb towards the microphone, then held his palms an inch apart to show the minnow of a tale he had to tell, then touched his watch.

'Must start some damned place,' said Sir Francis. 'What's the most important thing you know about his connection with me? There must be something to bring a man all the way up to this damned rock, hey?'

That there must, and not only one man. Pibble nerved himself for the bullying that was certain to follow the truth.

'Well,' he said, 'I know he lost his job at the Cavendish because of a disagreement with you. It changed his whole life, that and the war. He died when I was eleven. He was a ticket clerk at Clapham Junction. But even then, with his whole life spoilt, he was a very remarkable man. I want to know what he was like before the war, and what sort of person he might have become if things had been different.'

Sir Francis was laughing, but without a sound; rocking to and fro in his chair, mouth open, cheeks taut and purple.

'A ticket clerk!' he shrieked at last. 'No wonder our damned trains are still so hopeless!'

It was a Grand Guignol exhibition of nastiness – and no less fake than those tomato-ketchup horrors; the hard eyes were still watching Pibble, and he ploughed on.

'I doubt if even now I could understand what the disagreement was about. My father wouldn't talk about it, but my mother would sometimes bring it up. She used to say that he should have won the Nobel Prize, and he sometimes answered that she was wrong, but he didn't say why. She called it the Noble Prize, and I used to think it had something to do with the House of Lords. But since I grew up

I've imagined that he felt he had contributed some element towards the research for which you got your 1912 Nobel Prize, and you hadn't given him proper recognition.'

'Tchah! Damned melodramatic ideas all you laymen have. Nothing like that at all. Chap like your dad wasn't concerned with the theory, not one iota. His job was to build the gadgets to prove the theories – build what he'd been told and see that it didn't leak. Lab mechanic can be a genius, mind you – Lincoln and Everett both were, in different ways – but a genius at building gadgets. Brunel, not Darwin.'

It was at this point that Pibble remembered the envelope, clutched under his left armpit to leave his hands free for his earlier bit of dumb-show. He handed it to the old man, who clawed it open and drew out a smaller envelope, turning it over to study the big wax seal on the flap, so that Pibble could see but not read three words on the front in the familiar writing of the stolen MS.

Pibble broke the long silence.

'But you said my father was a great self-improver. I imagine that a man like that might have tried to follow the reasoning behind the gadgets he was building, and so might have stumbled on a usable idea.'

'Stumbled is the word for Will Pibble. Neither of 'em said anything about they should have been damned rich, hey?'

Pibble blinked.

'Come on, you nincompoop,' shouted Sir Francis. 'Doesn't mean anything. Everybody believes they should have been damned rich. I'm just trying to get you started.'

'My mother left all the money matters to my father, even when he was too ill to work and she had to go out. My father didn't think in those terms, I think, though he was a careful saver. When I had to move my mother out of the house I went through his desk, which I'd never done before, and I found several envelopes with small sums of money in them saying things like "Penny a day. Saved." "Sixpence a week. Saved." He never seemed to have much money, but I remember a holiday when his wallet seemed full of clean pound notes. He could have got a much better job, better-paid, I mean. He was clever by ordinary standards, and

86

very hard-working when he wasn't ill.'

'Ordinary clever people cause more bother than ordinary nincompoops. And you ought to know, with your education, that it was no use being clever and hard-working in the twenties if you were off sick half the time, like your dad. Now look here, you fool, you've got it all wrong. Your father worked for me right up to the day when I packed him off to fight for King and Country. We went through the Lab – I was a bit more senior by then, seeing I'd got my Prize – telling all the bright young fellows which uniform to go and die in. One chap, I remember, could ride a horse and of course he could do sums, so we detailed him for the Horse Artillery. Some of the mechanics were young enough, and I'd no use for your dad any more. I'd worked out that my line wasn't going to come to anything till there were millions of quid to spend on it, and that kind of tin wasn't going to be going with a war on. Tell you a rum thing – it's in my book – they set up one of the experiments I had my eye on at Harwell getting on for fifty years later. Lot of fuss in the papers – scum of the earth, journalists – saying it meant Free Energy for Everyman. Cost 'em four million, and didn't come to anything. I'd worked *that* out by then, too, on the back of an envelope. Cost me a ha'penny. But of course they wouldn't consult *me*, not any longer. Damned little sensitive schoolgirls, frightened I'd tell 'em what ninnies they were. And that four million came out of taxes *you* paid, young Pibble. I only paid my ha'penny, and then it wasn't wanted. What the devil are you staring at?'

Pibble shut his mouth, shuddered and managed at last to swallow.

'Can you prove it?' he whispered.

'I've still got the damned envelope, with the postmark on it, but what the devil has it to do with you?'

'No,' said Pibble, his throat still so constricted that it would only whisper, 'no, I'm sorry, it's very impertinent, but I meant can you prove my father worked for you until the war and left on good terms?'

The old man laid his ears back in the involuntary spasm of his rage. Hair and whiskers seemed to bristle like hackles. His cheeks puffed in and out. Suddenly he barked.

But the bark was laughter, the hackles fell back and he tugged the other end of his watch-chain out of his waistcoat pocket. It ended in an ordinary jeweller's catch which held a large, ornate gold seal whose die-surface was a purple stone cut with a crest. A curlicue of gold wire hung beside it.

'That's all I inherited from *my* dad,' said Sir Francis, tapping the seal. 'Sent it to me from Vichy. No letter, o'course. This is what I got from yours.'

He scrabbled at the catch with shivering claws, released the gold wire and passed it to Pibble. It was a simple semi-circle, with an eye in one end by which it had been threaded to the catch. The eye was tidily shaped, but looked as though it hadn't been there when the semi-circle had first been shaped and polished.

'It looks like half a wedding-ring,' said Pibble, getting his voice back.

'Damned sharp you think yourself,' said Sir Francis. 'Eighteen carats – I had it analysed.'

'I knew they had to postpone their wedding,' said Pibble slowly.

'Premature were you, hey?'

'No. It was just a remark I overheard.'

'O'course, o'course. Will Pibble was a damned honourable nincompoop, and it sounds as though your mum was worse. But he never had the grace to tell me he had a girl. Said he'd needed the gold for metal-to-glass seals – ingenious lad your dad was, in some ways – damned early on to that trick. No use to *me*, o'course. Gold melts.'

'Why did you keep it?'

'Because I'm a sentimental old dodderer, that's why. Put it on my chain when he gave it to me, never took it off. Suppose it expressed our relationship in a rum way. That damned chatterer Servitude talks about the noise of one hand clapping: half a ring's a good symbol, hey? First thing your dad looked for when . . . Tchah! Don't you brood on it, you idiot. If they'd gotten you earlier you would have been someone else.'

And that was true.

'Now look here,' said Sir Francis. 'I'm an old man, a'n't

I? Damned old by any ordinary standards. Old men have fancies, hey? Everybody knows that. I had a fancy to bring you up here and now I've a fancy to know about your fool of a father. You talk, I'll listen. Don't signify what you say – I'll get the bits I need.'

Pibble nodded and put the semi-circle of gold on the table. He touched his watch, held up the fingers of one hand and raised querying eyebrows. Sir Francis brooded a moment, shook his head, opened and closed one claw three times and then at the same time touched his temple and turned down the corners of his mouth in a harsh grimace. Fifteen minutes before he 'went soft'. So Pibble had ten minutes to fill with *Reminiscences of a Clapham Childhood*.

Sir Francis had his pad on his knee, but he wrote only once or twice while Pibble talked. Sometimes he snorted in derision, as when Pibble spoke of the non-flying kite. He nodded, unmoved, when Pibble described the Bartons' ailing lodger. Once or twice the eyes shifted up and sideways to where the microphone hung. Pibble himself spoke drably, telling the truth but toning down colours and blurring vivid edges. This was his own and private world, which only he should inhabit; why should this grisly old lizard be allowed to pry round it, just to provide pap for the ears of the holy spies? His voice dragged, reluctant.

Suddenly, while he was describing Father's experiments with dog-repellant in which to steep the trousers of their friend Cyril, the postman, Sir Francis made a sharp horizontal gesture, palm down, like a conductor cutting a fortissimo short. Pibble hurried the postman episode to its close.

'That's as much as I can remember for the moment,' he said. 'If you thought of anything which might open up other areas we could try again next time, perhaps.'

Sir Francis glared at him and said nothing. Pibble jerked his thumb towards the lurking mike to indicate that he was now wearing his conspirator's mask again.

'I imagine you'll be having your Gaelic lesson this afternoon,' he said. 'About three o'clock it'll be, won't it?'

Difficult to keep all the meaningfulness out of his voice

while suggesting this further plunge into melodrama. But it was the best place he could think of, supposing his interview with Brother Providence went badly, where they could settle their next move without this time-wasting code. Sir Francis nodded.

'I get old Dorrie to trot me out before my damned brain's properly clear,' he said. 'She gets her kicks out of babying me, and it gives me more time to make sense when I'm there.'

'So I'll come and look for you soon after seven, shall I?' said Pibble, shaking his head.

'Do what you damned well like,' said the old man tiredly. Only his eyes showed that the huge and selfish mind was still toiling in its office.

'I wish I could have been more help to you,' said Pibble. 'But I'm sure I will have come up with something by our next meeting.'

'You're a damned useless layabout if you haven't. Get out. Send Dorrie in.'

'Good-bye for now, sir.'

Sister Dorothy was still sitting on the step. No one else was in sight, but Brother Hope was probably at his niche below. Pibble squatted beside her in order to be able to whisper. At once she slumped her head on to his shoulder and moved it about like a dog nuzzling to have its ears scratched.

'Wake up!' he hissed. 'This is important.'

Her head came up and she looked at him with quick loathing.

'Get him out to the Macdonalds as early as you can,' he whispered.

The loathing changed, and the same sly and secretive look that he had seen when she brought the breakfast in slid over her face. She nodded, staggered to her feet and through the door, and began shouting. Pibble heard the words. 'Now I'm going to tell you what I think of you, you bloody bastard.' The door shut off the rest of the tirade.

He stood on the stairs, the echo of his own farewell running through his mind. He'd called the bloody bastard 'sir'. A change had come over their relationship and had now been formalised by his subconscious. At least at the rational level it made life easier, as he now had written authority, in the unmistakable handwriting, to do what he was going to do. Pity it contained that phrase about the pill – that was dangerous knowledge. He took the unfinished note from the pouch of his habit, folded it and tucked it into the elastic of his pants. As he let the orange cloth fall back into place he remembered that he'd left the half-ring on the table. He'd kept the paper but left the gold.

Ah well, that was a symbol too. First things first. Nothing mattered for the moment beside getting the old man to a fresh supply of cortisone in the next twenty-four hours, or possibly persuading the monks to resume the proper treatment. Pibble paced the cloisters, hoping that the peaceful rhythm would calm his churning mind. (A) There was this bloody old man, worthless apart from his genius, who had sent Father off to be gassed. And who, under the shock of the forged pill and the blatant microphone, had said all sorts of teasing little things, which would have to wait for thinking about. And who had kept for over fifty years half a wedding-ring given him by his victim. Without Sir Francis, young Jamie would have been some other child, growing up in some other town, perhaps with a well father. And that must wait, too.

(B) There was the Community, just as hateful, just as treacherous. At least there was no doubt now that Brother Patience hadn't been improvising placebos out of the school-room chalk. Pibble had never been happy with lawyer's law –the splitting of hairs long fallen from the scalp of justice – but this must be a deliberate attempt at murder, negative in its means but as sure and nasty as a sawn-off shot-gun. It forced Pibble to choose between his enemies, by giving him no choice.

There was no escape, and it wasn't going to be easy, either. Brother Providence would be a hard man to blackmail, bully, cajole, or even argue with on the rational level. And the first problem would be to save *his* face, and the Community's. Or seem to.

There were various threats he could wheel up, but fewer promises. So the threats would have to be carefully graded.

No mention of the book, at first. Certainly none of the murder. Assuming he won, were there any practical steps to take? Ambulance at Oban, in case Sir Francis stood the trip badly? Um. Supposing he didn't win, then it'd be a matter of stealing the boat, somehow, and in that case an ambulance might be a life-saver. If he won, they could lay it on by radio. If he didn't, they wouldn't let him. No chance of asking for it *before* negotiating – that'd queer his sales-pitch all right. But suppose . . . it'd be natural to telephone Mary, get her to pass on a piece of easy code to Tim: *then*, when the whole dicey charade was over, she could learn how essential she had been for the rescue of the finest brain in Europe . . . why, she might stay content with her lot for two whole weeks together!

Temptation comes in improbable shapes, but they have a family characteristic: the risks always seem smaller than they are.

Pibble stopped pacing, mind made up. Time to change into official-looking serge for the interview? No, he had paced too long, and if he didn't go to the office at once it'd be time for dinner. With mild surprise he realised that he hadn't been shown the office during the morning's tour. Why? Because it contained the photocopier, the one that had been mentioned after the reading of Father Bountiful's idiot postcard, the other gadget they needed a generator for. And why keep it secret? Because it had been used to copy Sir Francis's manuscript. Odd the way illumination comes, thought Pibble; not in steady drips, but in sudden spoutings after long drought. He wondered whether the process of scientific discovery was similar – toiling and toiling and getting no further, and then, almost in a dread, seeing a whole sequence of ideas like angels ascending and descending the ladder of logic.

He asked his way from the leader of a gang who now passed him, their pace subtly different, as though their limbs knew that the morning's hauling and lifting was over and that a meal, however dreary, awaited them.

A spiral staircase led up inside the wall of the Refectory to a large, light room, less plain than the ones he'd been shown but only because of the amount of brutalist office furniture in it: filing cabinet, steel desk, safe, steel and plastic chairs, radio equipment winking on a steel table against one wall, steel book-case against another, type-writer (a glossy electric toy and not the expected Imperial), and in the corner behind the door a shrouded object – the photocopier?

Three of the Virtues were in the room, and their attitudes showed that he had not interrupted anything, neither prayer nor gossip. Providence and Hope and the helicopter pilot had been waiting for him.

'Come in, come in,' said Brother Providence, rubbing his loose-skinned hands together with a noise like leaves swirling in the corner of a paved courtyard. 'I trust all went well at your interview.'

'Not too well,' said Pibble. 'I can't remember enough about the kind of things he wants to know. May I use your radio to send a telegram to my wife? She doesn't know when to expect me back.'

'You can ring her up if you wish. Father Bountiful saw fit to equip us with a radio telephone. Give Hope the number.'

Well, that'd make it easier still. And Mary would be home from her morning's bridge-school now, and setting out her ritual lunch of prunes and Fruti-Fort.

'You must let me pay, of course,' said Pibble.

Brother Providence looked at him coldly.

'Our style of life may have persuaded you that we are beggars,' he said. 'We are not.'

'I didn't mean that,' said Pibble, and wrote the number on the pad by the radio. Odd reaction from a man who had no feelings to hurt. Brother Hope settled down before the switches and indicator-lights and began to speak patiently with the mainland operator, his accent more Canadian than ever.

'Shall I have to explain to her about saying "over" and "out"?' said Pibble.

'Oh no, my dear lad,' said the pilot. 'This is a very fancy doofer indeed, just like Clore has in his Rollses. It transmits along one wavelenth and receives along another, and the other way round at Glasgow, where it connects

93

with mere vulgar telephone wires. You chat away like you do in your own lounge.'

'I understand,' lied Pibble.

Brother Hope seemed to have met an operator who spoke pure Gorbals; the combination of accents was making for misapprehensions. Pibble was nervy. To distract himself he watched the movements of gulls through a cracked pane; they were like blips on a radar screen, tiny in themselves but telling the eye significant things about the track of the enormous air.

'Is the wind always like this?' he said.

'It usually blows for a week when we get a good westerly,' said Brother Providence. 'But we do not talk or think about the weather as much as men do in Babylon. Did you listen to the forecast this morning, Tolerance?'

'No change, Prov,' said the pilot. 'And am I glad I'm not boating? *Truth*'s a sod in this kind of sea.'

'Ringing for you now,' said Brother Hope.

Pibble sat into the still-warm chair, and instantly crouched forwards to take his weight off his scraped buttocks. The purr of the ringing tone seemed strangely loud. It stopped with a click and the stolid voice answered. Pibble prattled gamely away.

'Hello, pigeon, it's me – I hoped I'd catch you. No, I'm still up here for at least a day more. It's a wireless joined to a telephone, but it's got two wavelengths so that you can speak and listen at the same time. Nor do I. Fascinating of course, but damned difficult too, that's what's holding me up. Of course I know he's old, ten years older than Father would have been – he doesn't pay attention for very long at a time, but he's astonishing while he does. It might be on the AA map, but it'll only be a dot, south of an island called Tiree. Cold wind, but very bracing. Of course I'm wearing them. Look, pigeon, this is very expensive – there are two important things. First, I won't be home till Friday evening. I'll ring again if I'm going to be later than that. OK, I'll write him out a cheque first thing on Saturday. Second, there's something I forgot to tell Tim Rackham at the office. Could you give him a ring? Got a pencil and paper? Fine. Just tell him there's no ban on ambulances at the

94

harbour. Got that? Yes, that's right. To-day, if possible. OK. I love you too. Bye.'

As he put the receiver down his chair was flipped round as if it had been caught in a whirlpool. He tried to yank himself into the room, towards the pilot who was sitting at the desk studying a scribbling pad, but his arms were twisted down behind the chair-back in an unbudgeable grip. His buttocks screamed with pain as he threshed. Straps bit into his wrists. Now he could see their heads and shoulders as his ankles were tamed. When they stood up Hope was perfectly unflurried, but Providence's beard rose and fell on his heaving chest.

'Was that enough for you, Tolerance?' he said.

'It'll have to be, won't it?' grumbled the pilot. 'If only Pa Bountiful had buzzed us a tape-recorder. Keep quiet, duckies, and listen to great art.'

He studied the pad and contorted his lips. An extraordinary, mincing, genteel series of syllables came from between them.

'Hello, pigeon, it's me – I hoped I'd catch you. No, I'm still up here for at least a day more. It's a wireless joined to a telephone, but it's got . . .'

'That sounds moderately convincing,' said Providence.

'It's only on the phone, mind,' said the pilot.

Providence twirled his bulk round to the chair, the drapery of his habit floating behind in coarse swatches.

'In Babylon,' said Brother Providence mildly, 'I used to give up Ximenes if I hadn't finished it in half an hour. An ambulance in Oban Harbour, Brother James?'

5

'Let me go,' said Pibble furiously.

The pilot immediately made another note on his pad.

Pibble tried to stand, achieved a quarter of an inch, and then had to endure the renewed agony as he sank back on to his ravaged buttocks.

'An ambulance in Oban Harbour?' prompted Providence.

Pibble said nothing. He knew now, and cursed himself for not knowing before – it should have been obvious – who the pilot was. Fish Benson, three-year escapee from the Scrubs, famed among the tall-tale-tellers of the Yard as the world's worst con-man. Providence had only told half the story: Fish had won his talent contest with imitations of TV personalities; and the ill company which he had been willed into was Farson's mob. Why, if he'd served his time he'd have been out last year, and very likely convicted and in again for some fresh outburst of naïve ingenuity. So here was another threat, maybe, in Pibble's strapped hands. And he'd never get anywhere if he didn't talk – no matter what raw material the pilot could mine from his arguments.

'I need an ambulance in Oban Harbour,' he said, 'in case Sir Francis doesn't stand the crossing very well.'

'It seems we have much to talk about, Brother James,' said Providence quietly. Hope nodded. Pibble felt a prickle of terror at the form of address, and squirmed.

'I'm sorry that in the circumstances we cannot make you more comfortable,' said Providence.

'I don't see why not,' said Pibble. 'You must know that my arse is bloody sore.'

'Dear me, I had forgotten. Is there a cushion anywhere, Hope?'

'Not since Father Bountiful left.'

'I got some dinky ones on *Truth*,' said the pilot, 'but 'tisn't worth the journey, really.'

'I still haven't grasped why you've seen fit to tie me up at all,' said Pibble more calmly.

'Ah,' said Providence with a tone of surprise that anyone could be so dense. 'Since you arrived in the island, Brother James, we have been vouchsafed three distinct signs: Sister Rita has had a serious relapse after months of steady progress across the board; Sister Dorothy has been miraculously drunk; and a well-cut stone has crushed the leg of one of our best masons. What can these be but warnings, warnings that Satan has entered Eden? Naturally our first duty is to capture and restrain him.'

'You forgot our mike conking three times,' said the pilot. (Three? All that code wasted?)

'I can't argue about the signs,' said Pibble, 'because that sort of thing seems to me quite irrational. Explain about the microphone.' He was getting pins and needles in his left calf.

'You did it in three times running,' said the pilot viciously.

'I mean,' said Pibble, 'why was it necessary to have a microphone in Sir Francis's room at all? He showed it to me last time I was there, but I couldn't have reached it if I'd wanted to.'

'Don't tell me the wetting done it in after all,' said the pilot. The underlying accent of his garage-hand days was beginning to show through the elbows of his stage vowels.

'A sign on the other side, I'd have thought,' said Pibble.

'Certainly not,' said Providence. 'But I will accept your ground, Brother James, and argue our case according to the logic of Babylon. Simplicity is old and tiresome, but he is a great soul, and there is hope for him yet. Furthermore he is valuable to us, not because he is rich, for he gave most of his worldly wealth to a worldly charity before he came here, but because he is famous.'

'Like I said, he's a good ad.,' said Hope. No laugh this time.

'So we have a duty to protect him,' said Providence, 'both for his sake and ours, even when on one of the silly whims of the old he contrives to send a message to a man he has never met, asking him to come here without any explanation of why he wants to see him. A normal man, with honest motives, would, on receiving such a summons, have got in touch with us for further information. He would certainly not have dropped his work and rushed north at once; nor would he have pretended when he got here that he was not a policeman. But the Lord looks after his own, and we were permitted to know that the man, from the moment he arrived, was attempting to deceive us about his job. And we were also permitted to know that he had a claim, though a very fanciful one, on poor Simplicity. A claim on what is left of his estate, which now, suddenly, with the publication of his book, is vastly enlarged. He is going to be a rich man again, and already the first of the hyaenas has arrived.'

'No!' cried Pibble, but his protest was not to the bearded monk. This wild illusion could only have come from one source – the sealed envelope. The old demon had betrayed him before he'd even come! Why? Why? Why?

'Yes, Brother James, we are not ignorant of the mean motives of Babylon. Now, we cannot protect Simplicity unless we know what has passed between these two men, so we install a listening device. The men meet, the device is working, and then suddenly it goes dead. The same at their second meeting. The third there is some doubt about. So we do not know what to think. Despite the signs that the Lord has sent we fear that we may have misjudged this man; in his direct dealings with us, he appears kindly disposed and intelligent for the most part; but we remember that he attempted to deceive us the moment he arrived, that his announced reason for coming here at all is unbelievably weak, and that at times he becomes both interfering and inquisitive.'

'Punished, weren't you,' pointed out the pilot, 'when you come nosey-parkering into our Reet's affairs?'

'Then, Brother James, after his third interview with Simplicity this policeman walks for some time in the cloisters, as if making a plan. Next he comes and asks to use our radio to send a message to his wife. In the course of that message he inserts a cryptic instruction to a third person which, if he had been acting with honest purpose, he could have sent quite openly to the appropriate authorities. Until that moment, as I say, we did not know what to think. Hope and Tolerance were against you, but I was inclined to be for you despite both your behaviour and the signs the Lord sent us. But now we all know what you are.'

'This is ridiculous,' said Pibble. 'All you've got to do is ask Sir Francis what he wants.'

'Of course we shall do that, but as you know there are several hours to wait before he can give us a sane answer. And the old are very easily influenced, and subject to whims which they afterwards regret. So we can occupy the interval by finding out more about you.'

'Tim Rackham is a colleague of mine at Scotland Yard,' said Pibble.

'One corrupt policeman will know others, Brother James. There are some of us in the Community with direct experience of this sad fact.'

'Not half,' said the pilot.

'I don't know how you expect me to think straight with my arse hurting like this and my legs going numb.'

'But surely there should be no need to *think*, Brother James. All you have to do is to tell us the truth.'

'Oh, rubbish. Of course I'll tell you the truth, but I've also got to try and think of evidence and arguments to persuade you that I'm not a crook and that you must let me take Sir Francis back to the mainland.'

'Alas for the weakness of sinful flesh. Perhaps we could slack his legs off, Hope.'

As the straps eased, Pibble squirmed carefully and found a tolerable position. Curious reaction from the three Virtues, or from two of them anyway. Hope seemed genuinely sad in his ruthlessness – sad, perhaps, for corrupt mankind, ruthless with corrupted Pibble. Providence also appeared to take his role at two levels: on the surface he was enjoying himself, purring his cool ironies, the voice of the Head pacing the dais before full school, touching his cane lightly with the tips of his fingers while he talks about 'civilised values' before calling out the boys he is going to beat; but that was just *manner* — underneath the elegant sadism Pibble could sense a sterner drive.

The pilot, by contrast, was straightforwardly happy with excited malice. Mustn't mention his real name, nor the stolen MS, nor the forged cortisone; push them too far and their mad self-righteousness would switch to madder self-preservation. Pibble felt he was dealing with spiritual psychopaths, unhampered by any legal or moral norm.

'Well, Brother James,' said Providence. 'We are waiting for your version of events.'

'The message about the ambulance,' said Pibble. 'That seems to be the main thing. I know Sir Francis doesn't like reporters – he calls them the scum of the earth. And I imagine you'd also prefer not to have a great fuss made about his return to the mainland. If I were in my office I could probably arrange to get an ambulance to the harbour without anyone asking why, but I couldn't possibly do so from here. The simplest thing is to get Tim Rackham to do it, and in such a way that the message doesn't go in clear through the Yard switch-board, which is by no means leak-proof. And of course it would give my wife a spot of excitement when she learnt what it was all about, which would cheer her up.'

Silence.

'If anything, I was cheating her, not you.'

Silence again. Pibble determined to leave the next move to them. His last sentence served as a warning against the delirium of confession, that curious condition in which tired, hungry and browbeaten prisoners talk and talk. Courts find it hard to believe afterwards that a man should have spoken so much to his own damage, and signed the statement as well. Men do, and now Pibble knew why.

'Why did you come here?' said Providence at last.

'I told you on the tower. I don't see how I can convince you that it is very important to me to know as much as I can about my father. He was a man of . . . well, of enormous moral stature, I believe, and now he's gone and almost forgotten, and I feel a duty to try and rescue what I can. His dealings with Sir Francis ended in a disagreement, or quarrel, or something – anyway it changed his whole life, and I want to know what it was.'

'You didn't tell me that before, Brother James.'

'It was none of your business, honestly.'

'It is now.'

Silence. Let him come to you, boy.

'So, Brother James, there is no question of your having come to take what you thought was your share of Simplicity's sudden wealth?'

'No. I've never imagined I had any claim on him at all. The first I'd heard of it was when you accused me of that five minutes ago.'

'Oh, come. It is a far more credible motive. To deny it discredits the rest of what you tell us.'

'Nonsense,' said Pibble. 'You keep telling me how much you know of Babylon, but if you didn't live so much out of the world – if you'd done thirty-five years of police work, as I have, you'd know that *any* motive is credible. Shall I go on?'

'Who's stopping you?' said the pilot.

'Right. I didn't say I was a policeman, because it's always simpler not to when one isn't actually on duty. I should think four out of five of my colleagues, when they're on holiday, simply say they work for the Home Office. I was asked up here by Sir Francis, and I came for perfectly good reasons. When we first met we talked for a little about my father – he wanted to make sure I was the right Pibble – and then he told me he wanted to leave the island, but that he thought you wouldn't let him go. Before he could explain any further he got too tired to pay attention. Next time we met there was a bit of fuss because a log had fallen out of the fire and the room was full of smoke, but when we'd settled down we talked again and I decided that he was fully compos mentis when he wasn't tired, and that he really did want to go. But I still didn't know whether there was any substance in his belief that you wouldn't let him, so I decided I would try to find out more about the Community before I saw him again. I didn't tell him that – I said I needed time to make up my mind. So I nosed around for a while – this is what you call being inquisitive and inter-fering. Of course I had to seem sympathetic. In fact I *am* sympathetic to certain aspects of your work. But inevitably I came to the conclusion that you would be likely to take an, er, rigid line about his leaving you.'

Long pause: no reaction. The pilot was picking his ear.

'In the interval I decided on a compromise course of action,' said Pibble. 'I wouldn't take him out with me, but I would take a letter to anybody he liked to name, telling them his troubles. He thinks his letters are being censored, and something you said suggested that there may be truth in this.'

'Something *I* said?' said Brother Providence.

'You said he *contrived* to invite me, but never mind. It seemed a fair course of action, and I was sure he was in no physical danger, even if he imagined he was. But the micro-phone changed my mind. It persuaded me that I ought to come and tackle you at once, and make certain proposi-tions to you. The trouble was that I couldn't explain any of this to Sir Francis, because we both imagined that the microphone was working; so we spent most of the time talking about what I remembered of my father from my childhood in Clapham. This rather upset me, as I feel, er, a strong antipathy to Sir Francis and didn't like him intruding onto areas which I regard as private; so I had to walk round the cloisters after our talk, simply to calm down and put my thoughts in order. Evidently I didn't calm down enough, because that's when I thought of the unnecessary com-plications about the ambulance. That's all, I think.'

The room became so still that Pibble fancied he could hear the squelch of the pilot's fingernail digging into a reluctant pocket of ear wax. Nonsense, of course, with this wind hissing through the gappy windows and dragging at the stonework.

'An ingenious construction,' said Brother Providence. 'Very ingenious on the spur of the moment. But it has a fatal hole in it. It is impossible to believe that you never spoke about Simplicity's book.'

Damn.

'But I told you,' said Pibble, 'that's why he asked me up

here in the first place – to talk about my father for use in his book. What else was there to say?'

No reaction. They simply stared at him as if he were a rat in a laboratory experiment.

'What propositions were you going to put to us, Brother James?' said Providence softly.

'Oh dear, I shall have to reshape them. I hadn't considered myself till now as a potentially corrupt policeman. They were going to be promises; now they'll have to be threats.'

'Same thing,' said the pilot. 'I know coppers.'

It was sinister how little he minded Pibble guessing about his intimacy with police affairs. Between the island and sanity loitered ten thousand indifferent waves, into any of which a poor swimmer might be made to fall.

'Put it like this,' said Pibble. 'I want to take Sir Francis (and Sister Dorothy, if she'd like to come) away tomorrow, without hindrance. I also want your word that you will arrange for Rita to have proper and regular consultations with a trained psychiatrist. In exchange I propose, rather against my own conscience, to keep quiet about a number of things when I get back to London.'

'What harm can your noise do to the City of God, Brother James? This is not Jericho?'

Providence was as calm as stone. All this had been foreseen.

'Well, for one thing,' said Pibble, 'I don't know how many ex-convicts are living up here, but I imagine that the probation authorities would like to know where some of them had got to.'

'My dear Brother James, I told you Servitude had excellent contacts.'

'Perhaps. But I can't believe that the Home Office – who are a good deal more on the ball these days than they were a few years back – would sanction your treatments of mental aberrants such as Rita, or near-deficients like St Bruno. Bruce, you call him.'

'My goodness me, is that all? I assure you, Brother James, the Home Office is delighted with the Community. We are keeping a fair number of habitual criminals out of trouble. Why, a year or two back there was a silly uproar about a Babylonish sect who called themselves Scientologists. We invited inspection then, and passed with honours.'

'What about the Town and Country Planning people?' said Pibble, pleased that his voice could still be controlled to the donnish level of the dispute. 'And the Ministry of Housing. And the local authorities up here. I can't really believe that you've permission to smother the island with a city twelve thousand furlongs each way; and suppose they don't order you to pull it down, you've still got a fearsome lot of re-building to bring what there is up to any kind of safety standards. I saw St Bruno using some very poor cement.'

'Ingenious, Brother James,' said Providence. He didn't look or sound as though a wrinkle of his visage had shifted behind the camouflage of hair. 'I'm surprised you haven't disparaged the quality of our drains – it would be consistent with your approach and I have always thought plumbing the dreariest of arts. But the question is academic now that you have decided to join the Faith of the Sealed and will not be going back to London.'

'I have decided nothing of the sort,' said Pibble, louder than he meant.

'Obstinacy, I warn you, Brother James, is a positive aid to our techniques. Be so kind as to fetch the seal, Hope.'

The square monk bent and opened a drawer in the steel desk and took out a bundle of the green sacking in which most of the Community was dressed. This he unwrapped with quick reverence. In the middle of it lay a lump of coarse black stone, which he handed to Providence.

'Hold his head, Hope, and you hold the chair behind, Tolerance, and then I shan't push him over. I regret, Brother James, that you are deprived of the ceremony of initiation before a full council of the Sealed. But I assure you that the ritual is effective. I have read that one of the so-called saints of the persecuted church in Rome, chained to the floor, yet celebrated the Communion of his church for his fellow prisoners by using his own chest as an altar. The Lord, in His mercy, disregards the poverty of the apparatus and sees only the central purpose. This will hurt.'

Pibble's head was gripped against Hope's muscular midriff. The chair was steadied. Providence held the stone before him, level with Pibble's eyes, so that the crude carving on its one shaped surface was visible – not the expected cross but a ladder. Providence moved in until the stone blurred with nearness, passed from Pibble's line of sight and pressed cold against his forehead. Providence bent below the line of his arm so that he could stare with cold passion into Pibble's eyes. He shifted his feet back until his weight was actually leaning on the stone. He began to speak.

'And I saw another angel ascending from the east, having the seal of the living God: and he cried with a loud voice to the four angels, to whom it was given to hurt the earth and the sea, saying Hurt not the earth, neither the sea, nor the trees, till we have sealed the servants of our God in their foreheads.'

The stone hurt. The ladder was pressing through the thin flesh of his forehead until the outer skin seemed to be rammed against the bone. Rubbish, and sadistic rubbish, thought Pibble, and stared firmly back into his torturer's eyes.

At once he wished he hadn't. There was power in that gaze which made it hard to look away. Besides, he was ashamed to drop his glance. Only his anger saved him from domination – not anger for his hurts or himself but for the whole of mankind, that anybody should feel they had a right to treat people like this. And Sir Francis was another of them, not giving a damn for mankind, packing off his only friend to choke in the trenches.

Armoured for the moment with this double rage, Pibble stared back into the tiger-coloured eyes. Providence was speaking again, chanting the words.

'Everything you have said today, Brother James, your lies as well as your truths, has told me that you are soft wax, ready for our seal. You are unhappy in your job, and your home life is evidently a wilderness, even by the standards of Babylon. Your avowed search for your lost father is manifestly a deep longing for authority. Here you will find it. The initiation is prolonged and painful by the standards of

Babylon. You must not believe that your colleagues, how-ever powerful, will come to your help; Tolerance can delay them indefinitely. We know your reputation in the police-force – nobody will be surprised that you have forsaken that endless grind to seek for God. During the time of your trial you will not know whether it is night or day; whether it is a minute that has passed, or a morning; whether you are awake or dreaming. Nothing in your whole universe will be certain except one single voice amid the darkness. That voice will be mine. For I am the messenger of the Lord God, sent to deliver you from hell, to guide you through the bewilderment of chaos, and to set your feet upon the streets of the Eternal City. We will begin at once. Unloose his hands, Hope, and take his watch off. Stand up, Brother James.'

The stone seal dragged at the skin as Providence took it away. Pibble stood dazed. He couldn't argue; he couldn't fight.

'Raise your arms, Brother James.'

He hesitated, then did so. It was best to seem beaten, and perhaps they would relax and give him a chance. Hope peeled the orange habit off him. For a moment he stood in his woollen underwear before the green and garlic-smelling sackcloth of his new uniform slid over his head. Hope unstrapped his ankles.

'We shall need a lantern at this first session,' said Providence. 'Will you fetch one, Tolerance? Be kind enough to follow me, Brother James. Hope will come directly behind you.'

The twisting stair gave him no chance to run, even if there had been somewhere to run to. As they came out into the cloisters Hope took his arm just above the elbow with one hand, and with the other twisted his fore-arm up behind his back. The grip did not hurt, but it would if his wrist were shoved an inch higher – 'enough to make an ape scream' the instructor had said at the crowd-control re-fresher course last autumn.

A school of green-habited brethren were trooping through the cloisters, on their way to a sparse meal fol-lowed by an afternoon of spiritual discipline. Their eyes tilted away from the little cortège that pushed against the tide, as though the ladder-imprint that still throbbed on Pibble's forehead were a grisly naevus which it would be rude to stare at. Providence led them up the passage towards Brother Patience's surgery; half way along he lifted a stout beam and opened a door on the right, one of the mysterious doors which should by all logic have led nowhere. Providence stood aside so that Hope could spin Pibble into the darkness with an effortless flick.

The three of them waited in silence, Pibble feeling the dankness of sunless flagstones strike through his soles and watching the grey rectangle of door where the two Virtues stood impassive. The grey changed its tinge and the pilot joined them with a smoky lantern.

'Like me to send your dinner along, Prov?' he said brightly.

'Yes, and Hope's too, if you please. And Brother James will need the usual tools.'

'It's a pleasure. No dinner for him, then?'

'He had Reet's egg for breakfast,' said Hope.

'Bags of protein there,' said the pilot with mock encouragement and handed Providence the lantern.

'Perhaps you would be good enough to fetch the microphone, Hope,' said Providence. 'I do not anticipate any violence.'

'A OK.'

When Providence pushed the door shut and carried the lantern into the room Pibble had his first chance to see the scope of his prison. A 'lonely cell' the builders had called it. It was a barrel-vaulted chamber, about eight foot square, containing nothing but a large, unhewn boulder in the exact centre of the floor; on this Providence sat, settling the lantern on the floor beside him so that half the cell was gold with its light and the other half black with his huge shadow.

'You are very silent, Brother James,' he said.

'One cannot argue with madmen.'

'You imagine that you can endure until your fellow-conspirators come from Babylon to rescue you?'

Pibble said nothing.

'Supposing you did, you would still be without hope. Simplicity has voluntarily signed a perfectly valid document – in fact it was his suggestion – making the Community his heirs and also the managers of all his literary affairs. You would return to Babylon not a penny richer. Worse, you would return with a ruined name – the name of a policeman who left his duty and rushed north on the flimsiest of excuses to pester a dying genius over a fancied claim on his estate, which he had already bequeathed to a respectable religious body. We live in an age which, I am sorry to say, is only too ready to believe the worst of policemen.'

'Dying?'

'Patience tells me he cannot survive long. He has a terrible disease. I was certain you knew – you came in such haste. I fear that your attentions may have hastened his death.'

Two green-clad brethren entered, the first carrying a platter of vegetable soup with two oatcakes at its rim, which he handed to Providence. The second placed on the floor a small log, an ordinary cold chisel and a fish-tailed bolster chisel. Both brethren made the ritual bow and left without a word. Providence began to spoon up his soup with careful slowness, speaking a few words between each spoonful.

'Our technique is perfectly simple,' he said. 'You must have read of it as it has been applied by other bodies for other purposes. We detach the imprisoned spirit from the material world, by removing it from any context it can understand. We give the material body apparently meaningless tasks, which are meaningful only in the logic of the Eternal City. We drill the material mind in an apparently meaningless catechism, which is meaningful only in the logic of the Eternal City. We detach the spirit from time, in the form of hours and days, and from any sensation save that of the holy stones. At whiles, but in no set pattern, we administer an excess of sensation in the form of pain – in Babylon they would call it aversion therapy. You may think it hard for well-meaning folk like us to have to torment our fellows, but it is not. I myself can endure the task without flinching, and Hope has progressed so far up the spiritual ladder that pain, of himself or others, is meaningless to him. So you will endure pain, but not as a punishment. You will be allowed food and sleep, as little as you need, but not as a reward. Your punishments will be spiritual and your rewards will be spiritual. You will suffer according to the will of God, and not your own will. You will be released from suffering according to the will of God, and not your own will. And you will eat, sleep, suffer and defecate in total dark.'

Pibble shook his head, as if to clear his ears of water. The spoon glinted as it moved rhythmically from plate to mouth, from mouth to plate. The light voice mouthed its repetitive phrases in a slow monotone, without emphasis, draining every word of its colour and texture. The effect was powerfully, and deliberately, hypnotic, coupled with the fear of the monk's threats and the pressure of his brooding personality. Yes, a weak mind, deprived of light, woken from irregular sleep to face meaningless torture . . . It was dangerous to say nothing . . . Providence put his plate down.

'Brother James, this is the last time I shall use your name until you are accepted on to the Great Board. Your work is valueless, your life futile. Your only hope is in our guidance. And we have more to offer than the spiritual gift of initiation. Our Community is expanding and we have need of another Virtue. The Lord sends us such rare souls when we have need of them, and I discern that yours, for all its wounds, may have been sent to this end. Now I shall instruct you in your task and teach you the first phrases of your catechism. Your task is this: you cannot be accepted on to the Great Board until you have thrown the holy Six, and you cannot throw until you have a die to throw; so in the dark you will cut the stone on which I sit until it is as square as a die. Cut it true, with God's help, and it will be the cornerstone of your salvation. The catechism opens with question and response. The first question is this: "Can you count the hairs on your own head?" And . . .'

'Only God can count the hairs on His own head,' intoned Pibble solemnly.

'Good, good,' said the monk without surprise.

'And he has none,' added Pibble. 'Or at least I shouldn't think so. I remember reading a piece by the Editor of the *New Statesman* arguing that God must have a sense of

110

humour because it is a desirable human characteristic and He must be endowed to a supreme degree with any desirable human characteristic. But so's a head, I'd have thought, and if you have a head it's desirable to have hairs on it, but I wouldn't imagine that anyone believed any more . . .'

'You will find that a sense of humour is a very undesirable human characteristic,' said Providence, rising heavily from his boulder. When he was half way up Pibble jumped him.

It was like an exhibition bout in the police gymnasium, with the right hand, moving apparently of its own free will, swinging horizontally in a perfectly timed curve to catch the big man between the jowl and shoulder. Pibble had always doubted his ability to deliver a chop like that without some fatal last-minute compunction which would abort the blow and leave his enemy angry but unhurt, like a wasp one has failed to swat. But now dislike and humiliation drove the arm and hardened the hand, and Providence, still unsurprised, flopped soundlessly sideways and lay still.

Pibble eased the door open and peeked out. He couldn't imagine Hope being caught and immobilised by a fluke like that; but the corridor was empty. Pibble shut the door and quietly lowered the beam into slots cut in the stone; then he nearly went back for the lantern – Providence deserved to come to in blank dark.

Supposing he *did* come to? But no bone had snapped, surely?

Patience's room was glazed with fixed panes, Pibble remembered, so he tried the door opposite him and found a store-room between whose mullions the big wind boomed unhindered. The sill was too high to climb to, but he dragged across a bale of the same coarse, green, garlic-smelling cloth as he was wearing and clambered up. He was crouched on the sill, balanced for the leap down into the grey grasses, when a hawk's grip seized him by the ankles, tweaked him back so that he didn't topple outwards, and dumped him on the bale.

This time he fought, for five useless seconds. Then Hope had him pinched in the old police hold, with his arm twisted fully upwards till the pain of it bit to the marrow of every bone. He managed not to scream, but by the time he was tossed against the far wall of his cell sweat had chilled all his surfaces until they were kin to the dank flagstones.

Providence was sitting up in the yellow light, rubbing the side of his neck.

'The mike's still dis,' said Hope. 'God told me not to try to mend it. You OK?'

Providence got to his feet, swayed with shut eyes, and then gazed at Pibble through three long breaths.

'Behold the man of blood,' he said. His speech was slurred now. 'How near damnation is he who will assault the servant of the Lord. How proud is that spirit; but it shall be led to humility. How vain is that mind; but it shall be shown its emptiness. And the leading and the showing are mine, for this burden God has laid on me. The blow is forgiven already, but the spirit shall be humbled, the mind brought to nothing. This man, Brother Hope, has undone many souls in Babylon. Many poor sinners has he humbled before the vain laws of Babylon. But now God has placed him as a counter on the board, and it shall be my hand that casts his dice, my finger that moves him from square to square, from ladder to ladder, from snake to snake, until he discovers the humility of stone and the patience of stone. As he has done to others, so shall he be done by. Now let us leave him to the mercies of the dark.'

Hope picked up the lantern and left. Providence picked up his plate and spoon, walked to the door, turned under the lintel and nodded. In that moment Pibble knew at last who he was.

'I didn't recognise you with the beard, Doctor Bray-brook,' he said.

The door shut. Outside came a heavy thud – not, alas, the sound of a big torso falling dead from a heart-attack, but the beam dropping home into its slots.

Pibble swayed in the dark. Now he was really terrified.

6

With precisely that turn, with precisely that nod, had
Doctor Braybrook, MA, DD, said his farewell to the world
when the policeman led him, grosser then, out of the dock
at the Old Bailey. A nod as calm and dismissive as if he had
been turning away on the expensive new stage of St
Estephe's Preparatory School after telling the assembled
boys exactly how far they fell short of the ideal of the
English Gentleman which it was the mission of St Estephe's
to produce.

Pibble crouched in the dark and started to work his way
across the cell, waving his arms like feelers before him.
Even in that position it was difficult to resist the instinctive
ducking of his head, as though the cell were suddenly full of
solid obstacles.

It had been a Fraud Squad case, but because of the
number and influence of the parents involved an officer of
known tact had been seconded to help with the blackmail
side; that had been Pibble. He had given evidence for four
hours, watched all the time by those unforgettable gold
eyes. And yet he had forgotten them.

His left hand found the boulder. He clutched it with his
right. It felt strangely slimy. No, that was the sweat on his
palms. He rested against the rock, knowing now that he
would have to find a lot of strength somewhere in the
crannies of his own system. He had, so far, endured or
drifted on the island with a curious fatalism. All he was
really interested in up here had happened so long ago, was
already fixed in time, that it seemed as if each minute of the
current day was equally decreed and fated. A dangerous

attitude, that, for a man about to be forcibly converted to a fanatical faith. So far as he'd thought about it, he'd done what he could with logical argument; now the insane tide of the Faith of the Sealed had obliterated all the landmarks of reason, and the only sensible course, it had seemed, was to wait till it ebbed and try again. Sir Francis had thirty-six hours-worth of cortisone. Pibble had been sure that in that time his captors must see that they couldn't get away with it. But now . . . if Providence was Braybrook, the tide would never ebb.

He stood up, unhunching his head by an effort of will. In about two hours Sir Francis would be at the Macdonalds' cottage. *They* might be persuaded to hide Pibble, and then in the night he could try to sneak back to the radio telephone. Or . . . But not unless he could get out; and the walls were two feet thick, or the building would never have stood. Digging took weeks. That left . . .

On the way back from the Common with his draggled and muddied kite under one arm, young Jamie had stopped to gawp at the Viaduct as a tank engine trundled a line of clacking trucks across it. Father's mouth was already open to explain, but Jamie was bored with the phenomenon of steam-power and forestalled him.

'But how do the arches stay up when they're made of such small bricks?'

So it had been the principles of the arch for ten minutes, while Jamie had teased at the rags of the kite-tail and half listened. Pibble could remember the smeary green of the tank-engine still, and the pink-and-white stripes of the tattered pyjamas which Mother had found to make the tail from, and the actual softness of the rotten cloth, and the smoky air and the smell from the paint-factory. But of all that earnest teaching only two sentences had endured:

'So you see, Jamie, an arch is like an egg-shell, and if you push it inwards you only make it stronger. Of course if you push it out, like a chick tapping at its shell, it's got no strength at all.'

From on top the stones of the barrel vault had looked smallish. Pray God that there weren't two layers. And that no sentry had been set, in the absence of the microphone,

114

to listen for his screamings and blasphemings. And that St Bruno's hadn't been the first batch of dud cement. And . . .

Curious, that. You could understand the inadequate tools as part of the dreary discipline needed to provide God with His broken spirits, but damp cement?

As he gruntingly tilted the boulder towards the side wall, waited for the thud of its toppling and stooped and felt to tilt it again, illumination struck him. The Community was broke.

Father Bountiful was being bountiful no longer, except in teasing postcards. The half-caste actress half way up Everest was now getting the benefit of the Hackenstadt millions. He had set the Community up with a beautiful boat unsuited to these seas, an elderly helicopter, brand-new office furniture, and the girderwork of an inane theology. But no steady income – that had depended on his continuing favour, which he had now withdrawn.

Fourth time, the boulder fell with a different thud as it settled against the side wall. Pibble levered it about until it stood stable, then crawled back on hands and knees, groping for the tools.

No need to ask, either, why Bountiful had lost interest; what else could happen to a playboy Messiah when a spirit as stern as Braybrook's comes to the Eternal City?

He missed the tools, and turned to begin a new sweep for them. At once he knelt painfully on a chisel; groping he found the little log and the other chisel. He crawled to the wall, stood and felt his way round to the door; there he knelt and prodded the fish-tail chisel into the crack between the wood and the threshold. Missing once or twice he banged it home with the log. Then he felt his way round the wall again to the boulder. At least the involuntary head-ducking seemed to be getting less. He climbed on to the rock, steadied his shoulders against the wall and with his right hand felt for the vault. As slow as a slug nosing through grass he moved his fingertips across the stone. It seemed to be all undifferentiated roughness to his touch, but in his mind's eye he kept the image of the fillet of masonry which had been inserted into the lopsided arch over the outer gateway; if they'd needed to fudge an important and visible place like that, surely in this hidden vault there must be half a hundred botchings. What he needed was a stone plug he could hammer out.

So Bountiful had dammed the freshet of Canadian dollars which once irrigated this spiritual desert. And that was the second time such a disaster had befallen Providence. The first time he had been Doctor Cecil Braybrook, all-powerful master of a machine which was going to restore the gentry of England to their former glories, make England itself a great moral force in the world again, and thus reform the whole round wicked world. Cruelly, the costs of running St Estephe's had gone up just as the supply of boys (suitable boys, of course) was mysteriously going down. Pibble moved his hand to another section of vault and marvelled at the instinctive way the monied classes preserve themselves; none of the rumours about St Estephe's can have started by then, surely.

His fingers were progressing in their new trade. They recognised a crack, a join, and traced it all round four corners. Too large a stone, but at one point they found a dried globule of cement slurry, which crumbled beautifully when he probed it with his nail. The neighbour stone was also hefty – ah, Crippen, this couldn't be the only section of the whole building fashioned from proper blocks! He let the network of joins lead him further down the vault, and came to a crack that widened until he could probe with his whole finger, as Tolerance had probed his own ear-hole, into the rubbishy bonding; and then the crack split, running down either side of a thin triangle, a stone wedge. Gingerly he lifted his left hand until the fingers of his right could feel the point of the chisel into the centre of the triangle; he nearly lost his place, and the tools, while he was juggling the log from his left to his right hand, but then he was steady again and able to tap the chisel-top with the log. He inched his feet round and found a position where he could really hit from, tapped at the chisel-top again to locate it in the dark, then swung at it, short-armed. Ouch!

Yes, that was Braybrook's style – vicarious sadism from lofty motives. At St Estephe's the children were encouraged to 'rub the corners off each other'. Here, by a further refinement, the victim bashed at his own limbs in the dark.

He practised until he could hit with firm blows. The angle was deadly tiring; the log was too light for such a purpose; his bruised hip nagged, and the moment he allowed himself to notice it his buttocks also clamoured for sympathy; the fillet did not budge. For a rest, and the comfort of feeling that he was making any progress at all, he edged the chisel down to the place where the crack widened and began to prod at the filling. Dust and fragments sputtered, and when he tried to shut his eyes he found that they were already screwed tight from the instinct of groping in the dark. The steel waggled gratifyingly into the cranny.

St Estephe's, founded to reform the world, a machine for making children miserable, smartish (which of the Royals had been tipped to go there?), presided over by earnest, jovial, scholary, rotund Doctor Braybrook – St Estephe's had run into shoal water. The new stage, the new swimming-pool, the new labs, all had cost more than Braybrook had budgeted for. He had resorted to fraud. With a true scholar's contempt for the world he had devised a wangle which was simple even by the simple standards of the City, and a merchant banker who was making the leap from Rumanian slum to heart-of-oak English Squirearchy in one generation instead of the usual three had spotted him at once. So had other parents, but Doctor Braybrook had proved considerably more adept at blackmail than fraud – he had their sons' whole future at stake, and the parents didn't know of each others' existence. What, risk young Marcus being turfed out of St Estephe's amid whispers of congenital depravity, and just when a Royal might be going there too! So young Marcus had stayed; and two parents had lent the school enough money for Braybrook to disentangle his fraud and devise, on the basis of his first experience, a considerably more plausible one.

The chisel jammed as the cranny narrowed. Pibble felt it along to the centre of the wedge, whanged with no result, felt it back to the tip and tried there. A heartening flake rapped the bridge of his nose. Carefully, exploring with a finger for results every few strokes, he began to knock the tip off the wedge. At each pause the skin of his fore-arm seemed to have swollen tauter with effort.

So Braybrook had bought calm for St Estephe's; but into that limpid interval had fallen a thunderbolt. The banker's wife had bolted, taking the executive jet, the pilot and the boy. The pilot, in a dither of lust and fear, had forgotten to check the fuel and the plane had ditched in mid-Atlantic, gliding down to the refuge of a chance sail – a lone yachtsman, trying to prove something, but now alone no longer. While the airman had sullenly steered and the boy had happily fished, the wife had kept the sailor away from his wireless, except for brief reports of his position – his navigational position – to his sponsoring newspaper. Then landfall, and a squealing press swallowed its tragic headlines in dizzy interviews during which many of the banker's private oddities had crawled into public view. The wife was a US citizen, with a passport green as a dollar bill, and though lawyers on both sides of the ocean took their usual pickings she kept the boy. The banker looked round for tender parts of society on which to revenge himself. He told the Public Prosecutor about St Estephe's.

Pibble eased aching shoulders against the cool stone and opened his eyes to see whether the dark was any less. It was not, but there was a noise in it – a faint hissing above his head, a tiny rattling at his feet. He moved his left hand in horizontal sweeps and held it still where the blackness tickled. Fine granules were pattering down, as if poured from a suger-sifter; he traced the stream up and found, just as the last grains fell, that all the cement at the thicker end of the wedge had simply fallen out, though he'd never even probed there. The wonder was that the vault stood at all. He thrust his chisel into his new gap and levered. The whole wedge moved. The long cranny at the other end gave him less leverage, but he managed to nudge the wedge the other way. And then back. And then forward. He bashed at the middle, convinced that he was nearly through. No go; the levering was simply shifting it a quarter of an inch on some hidden axis. Encouraged out of his aches he returned to chipping.

The rumour about the Royal had helped, but it was only when the case was under way that Fleet Street realised it was the Case. His Honour Judge Masham had always preferred a good ramble through the evidence, the more irrelevant the better; gradually and casually the extraordinary details came out. Pibble remembered the Senior Maths Master's evidence – he had helped with the sums, and didn't deny it. A youngish man, mumbling and shivering, a very bad witness. Judge Masham had lost his patience and asked how he managed to keep order in his class. You didn't have to keep order at St Estephe's, said the witness and his eyes flicked to the dock, where the accused nodded calmly. One of the things that had made the Maths Master so dithery was his evident belief that whatever Braybrook had done must, *ipso facto*, be right; and so the police and the court must be wrong – not mistakenly wrong but wickedly wrong. The boys had called Braybrook 'God', and though in every other way he had insisted on a fastidious piety, he hadn't minded about this perversion of the First Commandment.

Aha. A whole triangle of wedge, two inches deep to judge by the jolt of the chisel as it clove through, smacked down to the paving. Now his middle finger couldn't reach the bottom of the crack at the thin end of the fillet and could probe into the hole at the wider end as far as the second knuckle; the stone moved to and fro between these holes; he decided to try bashing at the newly exposed face in the hope of breaking up the axis point of the wedge where the larger stones pinched it. A twisted stance, but a change for some muscles, at least. He licked the salt sweat from his upper lip and bashed back-handed. All his torso was aching now, even while he worked, and his calves were as taut as a wet hawser from the unconscious effort to clutch his toes into their rough pedestal.

Not a scholarship school, St Estephe's. Braybrook, in the course of accounting for the elaborate lies in the prospectus, had claimed that he created character, not bookworms. Nor did he sculpt his characters with the cane – much. That was kept for an occasional favourite, some key figure in the termly initiation ceremonies which the staff 'knew nothing about'. A swishing from 'God' endowed the victim with quasi-priestly stigmata: those who had suffered at his hands were surely entitled to inflict on other boys such trivial sufferings as boys can rise to. But there were no suicides, few runnings-away. *Somebody* was keeping an eye on the children, judging their breaking-points with passionate detachment. So Braybrook, even while he juggled with loans, had toiled at his great task. He had got six years. It would have been four, the pundits had said, if Judge Masham had had a cheerier childhood himself. But there was no appeal.

The awkward angle told after very few blows; he leaned back, greasy with sweat and panting despairingly. Thirty minutes gone, say. He must see daylight soon, or there'd be no point in slogging on. As he leaned, a fresh shower of grit fell over the back of his head and down the inside of the collar of his habit, coating his sweat-dewed neck like sugar on a ripe strawberry. Too tired to swear, he felt for the source of the cascade. The large stone between the wedge and the wall must have shifted slightly and the cement along its nearer edge was pouring out. Not so good: the further it came down the more tightly it would jam itself in, and jam the battered fillet of stone beside it. He pressed upward, a grunting caryatid, but it was wasted strength. The thing was to try to *rotate* the smaller stone out of its place; but it was a wedge in two dimensions, downwards into the arch and sideways where the two larger stones had left a narrow triangle between them. So . . . He laid the chisel almost flush with the curve of the arch with its point against the remains of the thinner edge of the wedge, and began to tap it sideways. It moved, moved, moved, jarred, stuck. He bashed harder.

Six years for Braybrook then. Nearer four, with remission. He'd have come out two years ago, roughly – and in the meanwhile he'd have been visited by the absurd retired gunnery officer. Servitude would have been prison-visiting, under the mantle of some less peripheral sect; but later he'd have found his spiritual home, before Braybrook came out. He'd have offered Braybrook at least a hiding-place from reporters on this bleak rock – a place to go while

the world forgot him. That was a tolerable surface explanation; but Braybrook would have changed in prison, too.
His great work ruined, he'd have judged that the world was
not worthy of him, maybe. Also he'd have seen the extraordinary phenomenon, the almost pure power – pure
because it brings no privileges – which some inmates
achieve over the rest. He might even have achieved it
himself: *something*, and it needn't have been Servitude's
visits, must have sucked St Bruno and the safe-breaker and
the other ones whom Pibble didn't know up to this bitter
outpost.

Hell! The chisel jarred at every blow, achieving nothing.
Pibble explored with his fingers and found that the further
end of the wedge had retreated about an inch into the vault,
but the stone would now budge neither back nor forward.
He guided the chisel-point round to the other end and
began to bash upwards. Either he'd knock that corner off
or shove the whole thing through. Poor Pibble, you aren't
going to get out of here, are you, with your floppy wrists
and all your muscles feeling like plastic membranes filled
with warm water?

Rather than think about that, he thought about Braybrook again, knocking glumly at the stone as he did so.

The God-obsessed usher had come up here then,
changed but confirmed in his mission. And here he had
floated up through the hierarchy like a bubble rising in a
marsh, knowing that God had given him a great work to
perform. The Faith of the Sealed was a tool, he'd said on
the tower; not a perfect tool – more like the battered log St
Bruno had been breaking his rotten cement with – but it
was the tool which God had put into Braybrook's hands to
build his Eternal City with. On a more earthy level, Father
Bountiful's loopy interventions must have been even more
trying than the harryings of ninety sets of upper-bourgeois
parents. Or the four years lost had shortened Braybrook's
tract. For the millionaire meat-packer had skipped off to
his half-caste actress and communing with intelligent squid.
Pack it in? Not Braybrook, while there was the Lord's work
to be done and something to sell to do it with. Cracksman
handy, photocopier handy, St Bruno handy to forge the

121

necessary letters and contracts. All Sir Francis's mail could be censored; and if he guesses, why, he can be flushed down the everlasting sink in twenty-four hours by giving him chalk instead of cortisone. Packet of money in the book – six figures, probably. And no tax to pay as the Community was a charity under the meaning of the act. Crippen, thought Pibble, if they'd known I was coming they'd have flushed him away two days earlier. The old bastard's still not used up all his luck.

The jammed corner of the wedge gave, something cracked into his foot, and the stone began to rotate again as he tapped.

Braybrook/Providence. Providence/Braybrook. He had changed, he had grown a beard, but he had not forgotten. A spasm of terror ran through Pibble as he remembered the mysterious joke on the tower about the prison inmate who had recognised him, but whom he would not recognise. It would be a confirmation of the Lord's guidance if Providence were allowed to break one of the men who had broken Braybrook.

The wedge jammed again. Learned in its ways now he began to knock another corner off.

And the other Virtues would have welcomed Braybrook's coming. They all needed him: Servitude, the Aquinas of the outfit, seeker among crank creeds until he found one where any concept, however eclectic, could be bolted on the main structure – a creed, moreover, which encouraged frequent trips to Soho; Patience was a doctor who must have stepped out of line somewhere – overprescribed heroin, very likely – he'd the look of a man who has paddled in that Acheron; Tolerance, the ineptly named escaper, who'd found a sure hiding-place and enjoyed the playacting, the getting-away-with-murder, the power that the brainwashers have over the brainwashed; Hope – Pibble was afraid of Hope, physically afraid, but he admired him too in a dazed way – he might have been a saint, a guru, leading threadbare peasantries to resist the oppression of the Mafia or marketing instant peace in Hampstead sitting-rooms. His accent, and Braybrook's remark about Hope being the first of the Faith after Boun-

122

tiful, implied that he was a very early convert. Pibble remembered his melancholy in the office, the melancholy of a Holy Inquisitor putting aside his humanity in order to inflict on each comer the necessary agonies of salvation. Forgive me, Father, for I know what I do.

The wedge gave another half inch and a blast of light thrust at Pibble's dazzled eye. Blinking and weeping, he could see the precise point at which the stones pinched it; with the controlling sense of sight new born it took him three blows to knock it clean out of its slot. He stood and rested in that shower of light and for the first time dared to think about himself.

His heart slapped and thudded, rasping air whistled in and out of his larynx, his calves quivered and shuddered; his habit was dank with sweat and his hair clammy against his scalp; salt drops dribbled from his forelock, and when he wiped his mouth he found froth on the back of his hand. He had been working for a good hour in a barely controlled panic – not to save Sir Francis or Rita, or to uphold the honour of the Force – but for himself. Braybrook/Providence could have broken him in a fortnight, easy. Oh, not to mould him to a fully-fledged Virtue, fending his old life away as he strode towards his mad salvation; but to leave him a smashed creature, like the Maths Master in the witness box – useless at his job, quiet at home but given to shouted fragments of sentence between the silences.

On, Pibble, on. Nothing larger than a soul could slip through that slot of windswept sky.

The large stone which had delayed him by shifting inwards was still tiresome; it waggled, but not outwards. And now that he could see, he kept his eyes open and they were instantly full of cement-grit. All the aches of his body held a convention in the back of his neck, with the new effort of craning. He leaned out of the cascades of crumbs and studied the stone-work – if he could shift the big stone on the far side of the gap, then the even bigger one a course further up would be free along its lower edge. It came like a dream.

A nightmare struck him as he prevented it from falling through: Hope and Providence would be up there, sitting on the wall and quietly watching the first stirring of his stone molehill. He hesitated, then deliberately shoved the block upwards and saw with surprise, as his hands emerged into full light, that blood was tunnelling down the inside of both wrists. From above that'd have a grimly surrealist look – two blood-boltered arms lifting a stone upwards out of rough masonry – like that horror-story Simon Smith had told him about a South American earthquake, of a mother who had fallen down a crevasse and thrust her babe upwards as the crack had closed, leaving the dead projecting limbs and their living load.

Carefully he placed the stone out, standing on tip-toe and toppling it sideways until it rested where the dividing wall carried the arch. The long stone came as he touched it, tilting downwards, but he managed to steer it onto his shoulder where the cowl lay thick. When he climbed down to lower it to the floor he saw that fresh cascades of cement were streaming from all over the vault; he hurried back to his pedestal, and lifted out a large square block which proved heavier than he could hold so he simply let it drop with a jarring thud to the paving. He bent and found a suitable crack in the wall, where he drove in the chisel as far as it would go; his arm seemed to have no strength in it, and his palm was almost too tender to hold the log, from having gripped it so fiercely before. He put his foot onto the projecting chisel and reached for the top of the wall.

Suppose there were no tormentors waiting on the vault, what then? The radio telephone was in the office, with a locked door at the bottom and windows twenty foot up a blank outside wall. Not that he knew how to work the machine, and if he locked himself in to send a message they'd just disconnect the generator. The helicopter? Only in dreams was he able to fly that sort of gadget, and then it always turned into his old police bicycle before the plot was half developed. *Truth?* A sod in this kind of sea, the pilot had said, but at least he knew how to start an outboard motor, supposing the things were mended. Then round to the Macdonalds' inlet, fetch the old man from the cottage, and away! Or perhaps the Macdonalds could be persuaded to sail them home. Or . . . Come on, man, face the enemy.

He thrust himself up through the gap, diving for the sky. There were no watchers in the valley between the new storey and the old roof.

He had to rearrange his loose stones to get his elbows on the wall; the chisel, unsettled by this joggling, began to slide out, then clanged down to the flagstones just as he jerked upwards, wondering whether he could make it without using the other chisel for a second step. The panic at lost support gave his arms a moment of strength and before the metal had stopped ringing he was barking his belly on the masonry. He threshed with his legs behind him and unsettled more masonry from the arch – hell, someone would be bound to hear! The jarring and booming didn't stop as he wriggled round sideways to lie full length along the supporting wall. He turned to look.

Piece by piece the whole vault over his cell was giving way, one stone falling to loose another. He stared appalled at the mess and ruin, as small Jamie had stared appalled at the fragments of the big purple vase that lay in the brass fender when he'd clambered on to the piano stool to look at his face in the mirror over the mantelpiece and count his chicken-pox spots. All that painful work, in dust-smoking ruin. Something groaned in sympathy beside him, and he saw the new wall creak open. In a desperate baboon crouch he scuttered down the valley by the old roof. Fresh booming rose behind him.

He peered down over the edge beyond Patience's surgery, still half certain that somewhere he'd find Hope in ambush. Nothing but whistling grass, and beyond that the undulating heather.

He hung feet first. The tiles were clattering off the roof, and the wall now visibly bulging. With a roar like surf it slid down, filling the crater where the cell had been. Above it a bare beam projected, like God's finger in the cartoonist's convention, accusing. He dropped. Ouch! Little toe broken? No, only abused.

Of course. With the balancing thrust of his arch removed, the thrust of the next-door arch had shoved the whole wall inwards. Crippen, with a bit of luck they'd think he was under the rubble, judged by God. He put up his hood for extra camouflage and found that his sweat had brought out the garlic-smell with overpowering pungency; it was like sitting among labourers on the Metro. Bent double, he floundered towards the low horizon. No shouts rose as he scuttered across the skyline. He flopped into the heather and lay panting. Twelve, twelve-thirty, bit before one . . . say two o'clock now. An hour before Sir Francis was due at the Macdonalds' bothie. Carefully he peeked above the heather and looked back, half surprised to see that the tower had not come wobbling down in a chain reaction set off by the removal of that sliver of stone.

An unfamiliar area of his consciousness was reproaching him, amid all the furious chaos of pain and action, for not having noticed a less dramatically changed sensation. The moment he paid attention to it he discovered that the skin of his belly was no longer being pricked by the corners of Sir Francis's folded note – his written authority for all this derring-do. It must have fallen out from the elastic of his pants as he scrambled from the cell – if they dug for him and found it, they'd know he knew they were murderers.

All the same he felt strangely relieved to be acting again on no higher authority than his own conscience.

Back there, too, lay his other belongings. He must have scampered within ten feet of them. Police-card and wallet. Shoes and trousers.

7

He had forgotten about Rita.

There she was, foreshortened, kneeling on the floor of the quarry and knocking weak-wristedly with chisel and log at a faintly cuboid boulder. If his reactions had been actors inside the Little Theatre of his skull, their dialogue would have been written like this:

PIBBLE I $\Big\}$ *together* $\Big\{$ Poor kid!
PIBBLE II   Bloody nuisance
PIBBLE III (*slow-thinking, as usual*): That means there's a Virtue about, not counting Love! Tolerance and his damned valve-brothers.

She knelt with her back to him, but the lissom figure was recognisable, and the shining black hair, and the earnest ineffectualness. He lay on the lip of the quarry, too far along to see the launch or the quay; his heart was still knocking like an ill-adjusted diesel as he peered for a climbable route down that wouldn't bring him in sight of the quarry. So used was he now to the inert grammar of granite and heather that the intrusion of two humans and a dog confused him: he'd need ten minutes start, roughly, to get to the cottage. The odds on getting clear out of the harbour with *Truth* were sharply lowered. Rita was in an even worse case than he was for scurrying through the island's knee-high rubber shrubbery.

The stone-cutters had left a flight of stairs, four foot from

127

tread to tread, to his left. He worked his way down without a rattle and stalked up behind the kneeling figure.

'Countess,' he whispered, 'the time of our flight is at hand.'

She rose in a swirling flow. But the moment she saw him her cheeks lost their blush of romance, her eyes dimmed, her shoulders stooped, and she turned and knelt again to the dismal snicking of tiny chips from her stone. Chink, chink, chink went the chisel.

'Countess, the boat is ready and cannot wait.'

'I must cut my die. The stones are my brothers.'

'I come from my father, the king.'

'Our Father is king. It is for Him we are building the City.'

(So Providence had been talking to her in terms of her own Jeffrey Farnol fantasy.)

'I will cut your die for you, Countess. Chivalry demands no less.'

As he reached for the chisel she responded, letting go the tool and turning to him again with a heroine's eagerness. But the moment she actually faced him the fire died.

'Go away,' she whispered, 'or I'll call for Brother Tolerance and tell him all your snakes.'

She moved towards the lower lip of the quarry. Pibble snatched at her wrist.

'Wait,' he said.

She hesitated, and then watched, biting the back of a knuckle, while he grasped the hem of his habit and pulled it quickly over his head. If he was wrong, if the colour of the stuff wasn't a trigger for her madness, then he'd have to lay her out. He struggled out of the garlic jungle and stood before her like an advertisement for Officer's Woollen Underwear from an Army and Navy Stores Catalogue before world wars had been thought of.

'My Prince!' she cried, and flung to him, thin arms grappling round his weary neck, soft lips sucking at his face in crazed kisses.

'Keep chopping, sweetie,' sang a tenor voice from the quay. The wind carried it, but with luck had thinned Rita's cry to a bird-call; Pibble ducked out of her clutch, picked up

128

the tools and renewed the chink-chink-chink. With his head he motioned her to kneel beside him.

'Your Highness,' she whispered, 'forgive me. I did not know you in your disguise.'

'My father is disguised also. Will you carry a message to him?'

'I will treasure it in my heart,' she breathed.

'You will know him because he is very old, and hairy. It is part of his disguise. Go through the heather to the cottage which lies under the headland at the north end of the island –' he pointed '– and either you'll find him there or else he'll be expected soon. Soon expected, I mean. The women in the cottage do not speak our tongue. My father may pretend madness, but tell him that I follow you, with all speed. Speak of me by the name I use when in hiding – James Pibble.'

'James Pibble!' she whispered, with a gesture of courtly amusement. 'How too delicious!'

'Go now,' said Pibble. 'Keep the wind to your left and try not to be seen from the, er, castle. You can climb the cliff there.'

He pointed to the blocks by which he had clambered down. She sped across the quarry floor, turned and waved with gay bravado, and clambered lightly to the top. Pibble, watching while he clinked at random at the boulder, was interested to see how cunningly she slid over the skyline. He tried to remember that long-ago course in abnormal psychology: should you, in Braybrook's words, answer a fool according to his folly? Or was the next verse of the Book of Proverbs, which gives precisely the opposite advice, more relevant? Was he making her madness better, or helping her to wallow further into it? Would her fantasy sustain her slight strength as far as the cottage? It was uncanny to be able to play on her aberrations like that, and nastily pleasurable – Pibble realised why Braybrook hadn't minded the monied striplings calling him 'God'.

He picked up a stone he could carry one-handed and, clinking at it spasmodically with the chisel, crept to the edge of the quarry.

The pilot was busy with his engines. The port one seemed

129

finished, but judging by the pieces on the deck there was still work to be done on the starboard one. Hell! There was no point in trying to steal *Truth* now – he wasn't mechanic enough to finish putting a big motor like that together. But the pilot was; even if they got away in the Macdonalds' boat, a crew of monk-thugs could come hurtling after them.

He clinked his way back to Rita's boulder and knapped the best-formed corner off it with a dozen solid blows. He was cutting anti-dice – a notion which gave him strength to demolish another protuberance which might stop the thing from rolling. When it was off he trundled the boulder towards the chute and bashed away at the corners on its other side. The sweat in his woollens was evaporating, chilling him in the steady wind. He picked up his habit, then put it down again as his nostrils caught the reek of it. Where was Brother Love? The brown habits had smelt of mint, the orange one of nothing much and the green ones of garlic; and the Great Dane had first made friends with him in the colour-obliterating night, after sniffing deliberately at his chest.

Clink, clink, clink. Tumble stone again. It was neither round nor cuboid now, and trundled fairly well. Knock that corner off. Tumble again. Five minutes since Rita left, say. He left the boulder at the top of the chute and scuttled back across the quarry floor to where the last big bite out of the hillside had spilt a scree of rubble. God seemed to have abetted the monks in their madness by giving them an island whose rock-base was already fissured into rectangular sections; Pibble had to hunt to find two roughly round stones, about the size of a man's skull. He carried them back to the top of the chute one by one, clinking at them with the chisel as he went. Ah well, might as well start now. Either the pilot would come up and fight him, which would be nasty, or he'd run back to the buildings for help, which would give Pibble ten minutes' start – more if they didn't guess at once where he'd gone. If he was dead lucky he'd be out of the quarry with the job done, before the pilot came up, and they'd think Rita was the villain, and with the chaos back at the buildings . . .

He trundled Rita's boulder the last two feet to the lip of

the chute and stared at slope and angles for the last time before he committed himself: there'd be no chance, surely, of it bouncing so high from the quay that it would clear the transom and squash the kneeling man. Odds were it would smash into the stern or batter the propellers. He gave the rock a heave to set it rolling.

The chute boomed. Tolerance looked over his shoulder and shouted. The boulder bounced and bounced again, and all the timber thundered. It hit the cobbles of the quay with a sharp crack, but landed on a corner and spun sideways, in an off-break, bouncing high and curving down to clip the corner of *Truth*'s stern, making the whole boat plunge at its moorings like a tethered mule, before falling into the harbour with an oddly undramatic splash.

As Pibble picked up his second boulder and started it down the chute the pilot was running for the gangway. This stone was smaller and went down with a different motion, leaping high where the flexing of the bottom planks sprung back beneath its weight. Pibble bent for his third stone, and straightened in time to see the pilot come hurling round the corner of the quay as the second one reached the bottom. It looked as if it would run true for the port engine, but the pilot, like a full back desperately defending a goal-line behind a sprawling keeper, thrust one brown-swathed knee into the path of the stone. After the thunder of its bounding down the timber the noise it made as it crushed his legbones was a momentary light pattering. He flung up his arms as he fell, shouting. Not a scream – a word. 'Love!'

The stone, unhindered by the pitiful obstacle of flesh, crunched into the engine with a tearing clang. Pibble took his last missile off the chute, tossed his habit down to the quay, and started to work his way down the splintered timber, gripping the sides with his hands and shuffling his feet six inches at a time down the steep pitch. The man at the bottom lay still, his left arm dangling over the quayside, his head on the verge. The dog, come from nowhere as silent as nightfall, stood above him, licking his face with slow, tender strokes. They made a pathetic group, as though Landseer had posed them for an attempt to cash in on the Oxford Movement.

Pibble began to skirt the pair on his way to the boat, but stopped when he saw how dangerously close Tolerance lay to the edge. One groaning move as he came to would pitch him fatally over. He walked firmly towards the pair. The dog looked up.

'It's OK, Love,' said Pibble quietly.

The dog stood to one side, its tail not really wagging but twitching slightly with relief of having a human to take responsibility for an event outside its training. Pibble lifted Tolerance by the shoulders and pulled him a few feet towards safety. The effort made him realise how much of his middle-aged strength was spent. Watched by the dog he fetched his habit from below the cliffs and spread it across the body as a slight guard against the killing chill of shock.

Love's hackles rose. He padded stiffly in and straddled the unconscious man. Pibble realised his mistake and darted in to whisk the habit away. The creamy teeth bared in a deep, purring snarl and the mask slashed wickedly round. Pibble backed off, walked along the quay and up the gangway, picked up the cylinder head from the deck and threw it into the harbour. As he passed the man and the dog on his way back to the helicopter shed, the pilot opened his eyes.

'Oi, Love, have a good kip then? Lemme get up, mate.'

Speaking to the dog his accent was unaffected; garage, not stage. The dog snarled.

'Oi, Love, it's me! Tolly! Where's that sod of a copper, then?'

The snarl deepened.

'Cut it out, mate! I've hurt my leg.'

Neither of them seemed to notice as Pibble slipped past. The door of the shed was held by a thick, looped chain, fastened with a newish padlock. He'd planned to remove a distributor-arm, if he could find it, so that only he could make the gadget fly, but with the door locked and the pilot out of action it wasn't possible or necessary. Crippen, if only all decisions were as clear-cut! He climbed awkwardly up the chute, scared of every splinter. The dog's attitude had changed, subtly. Tolerance was still talking, and the coaxing murmur of his voice droned up on the big wind.

Love was puzzled already. It wouldn't be long before Tolerance – supposing he didn't faint with pain – chatted him out of his Pavlov-induced savagery, or else worked out what had happened to change his nature and twitched off the green habit to expose the mint-smelling, dog-enchanting cloth below.

Pibble struggled up the ogrish staircase he'd descended. It was like dream gymnastics, with all limbs lolling and all holds wrong. His hurts were badgering him again for sympathy and comfort. At last he rolled over the skyline and crawled down among the scattered boulders. The buildings were visible from this slight rise. He could see a figure or two on the vault which led to his shattered cell. One pointed, but inwards. They had their backs to him. He scampered down the slope, thinking how conspicuous a running man in woollen underwear must be amid the grey grasses or the russet and purple heather. From lower in the dip only the top of the tower still showed, and Braybrook didn't seem to have set a watcher there – he'd be all right if he kept as far as possible to the hollows, though it would take him longer then to reach the doubtful haven of the Macdonalds' cottage. If only the Community had kept sheep, he could have passed from a distance as just one more woolly object on the landscape, browsing erratically north.

He walked on, stepping high like a dressage horse. The dip he was in curled away eastwards until he had to edge up the left-hand slope, glancing over his shoulder every few paces to see whether the buildings were in sight again. The tower rose higher each time, sinister but untenanted. As soon as the first roofs showed he dropped to his baboon posture and lurched on. Soon he had to go on hands and knees, then on his belly to wriggle over the crest through the shielding heather. His breath shrilled in his throat, but he went down the far side in a wallowing gallop, tripping twice to tumble into springy heather.

This side of the island was a series of ridges and valleys; walking the other way that morning he had been aware of them only in the graph-curve of the cliff-tops; now he found how far they ran inland. Every two hundred yards he had to

133

repeat the tiresome and tiring series of gaits from valley to ridge to valley: stride, crouch, crawl, wriggle, gallop. One valley contained a bog which he'd missed on his route along the cliff – black, acid, and stinking-sweet. He squelched heedlessly in before remembering tales of bogs that had swallowed wagon-trains, but the ooze never rose above his ankles. Even while he was wriggling over the next ridge the slime of it clung, strangely refreshing, to his feet.

Two ridges beyond that he reached the long slope which rose through the vanished village to the Macdonalds' cottage. The mad collie scratched in its doorway; gale-shredded smoke from the roof suggested life inside. Boozy with self-pity Pibble lurched towards it, wondering how he could ever have placed any hope in this hopeless refuge. They should never have wished all this on him, this bashing and careering with no play anywhere for ordinary stolid logic. They couldn't ask a man – a quiet, civilised, diesel-breathing man – to endure and cling to this piffling rock while the waves of unreason threshed over him. They were trying him out, they wanted him to break, they . . .

They?

He glimpsed the panel, the inquisitors, through a rift of mind-fog. Braybrook was there, gold-eyed, and Sir Francis, and Father in his plus-twos, and . . .

The last time he fell his hands slapped on to ancient cobbles, all displaced by roots and sprouts of grass and heather. He got up and stood swaying; the cottage was only fifty yards up the invisible street. His feet and shins were scarlet with the slashing heather, but the bog-slime had been brushed clean away except in the crannies between his toes.

The collie yelped towards him, taut on its many-knotted rope, but before he could start to circle round beyond its reach in the hope of coming to a back window, a brown arm poked through the door and jerked at the rope; the collie stopped its clamour in mid-yelp and trotted back to the doorway to complete its scratching. It didn't even glance up as Pibble passed beside it.

'Who are you, you damned fellow?' creaked a voice from the dimness, a dull voice without a brain behind it.

'It is the Prince, Sire,' fluttered another, 'in his new uniform.'

A monotonous snoring rose from ground level.

Pibble groped away from the door, and with the main light no longer falling from behind him he could see. Sir Francis sat in a rocking-chair, hands crossed on his walking-stick, arms poking out from a complex of cloaks and shawls, eyes staring without interest at the light that came through the door, as a new-born child stares at the brightest object in its vision. A square brown parcel lay on his lap. Either Pibble was early and his period of genius was not yet on him; or he was late and it was over. Rita sat at the old man's feet, smiling her uncanny smile. Two grey-haired weatherbeaten women – the ones he'd seen gutting herring that morning, were peering at Pibble through narrowed eyes, as if he were a portent of a storm.

'Mo chreach!' said one. 'S fhada nach robh sex maniac againn 's an eilean!'

'Ged a bha doighean,' said the other, 'gu math eibhinn aig brathair do sheanair na latha.'

They lifted their aprons a fastidious inch and walked to a position where the rough table stood between them and the intruder; the fatter one picked up a gutting knife and felt its blade.

'I'm Pibble, sir.'

'Come with another of your damned messes to show me, hey? Let's have a look at it.'

Pibble could think of no answer to this sleep-talking out of another era. The dead voice droned on suddenly.

'Solidifier? Damned rubbish. Two damned waxes will melt as easy as one.'

'Your father has pretended madness since I came,' said Rita. 'And see, his attendant is most amusingly pretending drunkenness. I admire her loyalty, Your Highness, more than her taste.'

The snoring came from beyond the table where Sister Dorothy lay on the bare earth floor, mouth open, face purple.

'Do you speak any English at all?' said Pibble.

'Put it in the cupboard,' said Sir Francis. 'I might think of a use for the damned stuff.'

The Macdonalds shook their heads at Pibble. The fatter one put the knife back on the table, but neither moved from behind its protection.

'Pibble!' barked Sir Francis. 'What are you doing in that idiot attire?'

'Thank God!' said Pibble.

'Got someone to think for you now, hey? Where's Dorrie?'

'The other side of the table.'

Sir Francis craned to look.

'Damned dipso,' he snarled. 'Brought her here to get her off the stuff, and what does she do but persuade these idiot women to use their old still?'

The Macdonalds cackled an incomprehensible protest at the recognised word. Sir Francis turned and spoke to them in Gaelic, quite gently and slowly. They smiled and curtsied, and one turned and started to rummage in a splintered tea-chest by the wall.

'Well, man, how are you going to get us off this damned island, hey?'

'I tried to talk reason to Brother Providence, but he shut me up in a cell and started to brainwash me . . .'

The old man snorted and grinned.

'I think I could have persuaded some of the others to see reason – the doctor, Patience, for instance. But Providence is beyond argument. He thinks he's God. I knew him before, when . . .'

'Don't waste time telling me. He used to be a damned usher at a nobby crammers, then they put him in clink.'

'If you knew that,' said Pibble slowly, 'why did you trust him enough to let him have a letter telling him who I was?'

'Course I didn't trust him, you blazing ass, any more than I did you. I put my seal on it.'

'A hot knife . . .' began Pibble.

'Stop wasting time!' screamed the old man. 'Haven't I had enough damned trouble with Pibbles and seals? They've tried to kill me and they've tried to shut you up. Now it's your job to get me off the island.'

'Can you persuade the Macdonalds to lend us their boat?'

'Your cronies in brown will come after us,' snarled the old man.

'I put their launch out of action,' said Pibble, 'and I broke the helicopter pilot's leg.'

'That fat one can fly,' said Sir Francis. 'He used to be Hackenstadt's chauffeur.'

'I don't see what harm they could do us from a helicopter, once we're at sea,' said Pibble. 'The only other thing I can think of is to hide out until I can get to the radio telephone and ask the mainland for help.'

'No hope of that, you damned idiot. They take a couple of valves out when they aren't using it, in case any of the other ninnies tries to get in touch with someone sane. Damned ironic, hey? You, girl, take my spat off.'

He thrust out a foot. The spat was the palest violet. Rita unlaced the strap with obsequious fingers and passed the garment up into his mittened hands. He scratched in his waistcoat pocket and brought out a fat, many-gadgeted old pen-knife, with whose scissor-device he picked at the stitching of the spat until he could put both index fingers into the slit.

'Get dressed, you gawping ninny,' he grunted as he tugged with surprising power at the cloth. Pibble saw that two grey jerseys and a pair of dun-coloured trousers lay on the table and a pair of calf-length gumboots stood beside it. The woman was putting more clothes back into the tea-chest. Pibble dressed, wondering what was so ironic about the monks' security precautions over their radio, and watching Sir Francis squeeze coin after coin into his lap.

'Cousin of mine,' croaked the old man, 'stupid girl, volunteer nurse, got caught in Serbia in 'fifteen. Prisoner of War for a year. By the time she was exchanged, things had got damned primitive. A reel of cotton sold for a sovereign. Plenty of sovereigns, see, and damned little else. All their mammas had made 'em sew gold into the lining of their petticoats. Good thing for British virtue the guards never found out, hey? But a damned good notion – I've carried a

137

bit of gold about ever since I could spare it.'

He turned and spoke again to the Macdonalds. The slowness and meekness of his Gaelic, Pibble now saw, didn't come from any respect for them but because he was not at home in the language. They looked worried. One spoke. He counted twelve of the coins out on to the table. The thinner Macdonald picked one up and carried it over to the door, where she peered at it and then bit it. The other one spoke with her in the soft, brushing syllables of their own language, then they both turned to Sir Francis and shook their heads.

'Chan fhaigh, gu dearbh,' said the more vocal one.

'You could tell them what my job is, sir. They'd be in trouble if we told the customs about their still.'

'Blackmail runs in the family, hey?' snarled Sir Francis.

He spoke again in Gaelic, and Pibble caught a word which might have been 'police'. The Macdonalds flicked their eyes towards him, and away. Sir Francis put three more sovereigns on the table. They nodded unhappily.

'Done that for you,' grinned Sir Francis. He was blatantly pleased with the excitement, his adrenalin busy. Crippen, would that mean he was using up his last pill faster? Pibble tried to phrase his next question carefully.

'I think it's about forty miles, sir.'

'Sixty by sea, nincompoop.'

'So if we leave now we ought to be there in twelve hours or so.'

'What of it?'

No good, except that the old demon knew what he meant and wasn't worried.

'Would you ask them if there's enough fuel on board, sir? We don't want to get stuck half way.'

'Fuel, hey?'

'Yes. Petrol or diesel or whatever they use.'

Crippen, was he going soft already?

'There's no damned engine in that boat, Pibble. She's gaff-rigged, loose-footed, and you're going to have to sail her home.'

'Sail her?'

'Sail her, Pibble. My saints, but you remind me of your

138

damned dad! Done any sailing?'

'No, sir.'

The old man tilted himself forward from the rocking-chair until it looked as if he'd go sprawling across the floor. He caught himself deftly on his stick and was standing, still clutching the parcel.

'You've got twenty minutes to learn, then,' he said. 'No wonder the damned police never catch anybody.'

He spoke again in Gaelic and tossed his last coin on to the floor. One of the women fetched more clothing while the other brought out of a cupboard a flat, dark loaf and a bottle containing a liquid paler than oat-straw.

'Couldn't the Miss Macdonalds sail us over?' said Pibble. 'That way they'd get their boat back sooner.'

'They're Mrs Macdonalds,' snarled Sir Francis. 'Married the same man. Genius he must have been to commit bigamy on an island this size. But the damned fool got himself torpedoed during the war, and they're still waiting for him to come back. One can't leave the other, for fear he'll come when she's away. They can't go together, because then they think the brown brothers will come and pull their house down to build the City with. That's where the rest of the village went. These two are loopy, Pibble, loopy with loneliness. I've done damned well to wheedle the boat off 'em as it is. You carry Dorrie and the food. This ninny of a girl can take the spare clothes and help me.'

'Countess,' said Pibble, 'my father is weary with age. Would you lend him your shoulder while we walk to the boat?'

Rita rose from the floor in a swift curtsy. 'I am His Majesty's servant to command. With my life if need be.'

Sir Francis peered at her, snorting.

'Another loony, hey?' he shouted.

'My father pretends madness again,' explained Pibble.

'It is His Majesty's pleasure,' simpered Rita, as sweet as barley-water.

'Three loonies, one drunk, and a bone-headed peeler!' exclaimed Sir Francis, raising his whiskery old head towards the God he had dispensed with. He bowed over his walking-stick.

'Giddap then, m'lady,' he croaked. 'All the countesses I've known have been a damned sight older and uglier.'

Rita's sick smile flashed at the compliment.

'You carry the clothes in your left hand, my beauty,' he said. 'You'll need 'em, and so will Dorrie. That'll leave your right side free to help me.'

Rita tucked the bundle of oily wool under her arm, then moved to the old man's side and drew his free arm over her shoulder.

'She's not all that strong, sir,' said Pibble. 'She's been very badly treated.'

'So've I, dammit,' grumbled Sir Francis and hobbled through the door.

Pibble walked wearily round the table and hauled at Sister Dorothy's limp wrists until she flumped into a sitting position. He knelt, dragged her torso across his shoulder with his left hand and slid his right hand through the hampering folds of habit until he could grip her by the right thigh. Her snoring did not cease, but slowed and deepened a semitone. He knew his stomach muscles would never be up to lifting her.

A cackling broke out above his head and he felt his ribs being prodded. Craning from beneath Sister Dorothy's armpit he saw the Macdonalds making signs at him. The fatter one bent and held the shoulders so that he could stand again. The other bounced sprightly on to the table and sat there, legs dangling, head hanging. She emitted three convincing snores, then nodded brightly to Pibble and pointed to the inert mass of Sister Dorothy. Pibble nodded too. Yes, he might just manage it that way.

The thinner beldame went to the wall and poured water from a big pitcher into an enamel mug, which she gave him. The water was sweet, pale brown and almost magically refreshing. The Macdonalds nodded and smiled while he took a second mug; when he was not gulping the stuff down he realised that most of the taste was not fresh natural sweetness of peat-water but a good lacing of home-made whisky. Cunning old harridans! Suborning a police officer. He smiled, and they smiled back with peasant-cunning eyes.

140

Even with the three of them there was a tedious amount of heaving and dragging before they had the drunkard on the table; but once they'd settled her there the fireman's lift became a practical proposition. Pibble grunted as he took the weight, stood upright, jerked his shoulder to settle the soggy body to a better posture, and staggered towards the door.

The cackling broke out again and wearily he turned. The fatter Mrs Macdonald was holding the food-bag towards him; he took it. The thinner one began to speak to him in Gaelic, tragic, pleading, earnest. When she finished he nodded and smiled, as though no torture on earth could have drawn from him the secret of their experiment with alcohol. Once more he staggered towards the door. He eased his burden through, bent-kneed.

The wide light of the headland dazzled him like the glare off a snow-field. He had been longer than he meant. Rita and Sir Francis were already out of sight round the abrupt shoulder. Pibble plodded after them with small and straining steps, blessing the diet that had kept Sister Dorothy leaner than civilised food might have made her. Suddenly the hiss of the wind and the creaking of the gulls vanished beneath a nearer noise – the collie's maniac yelp. He swung heavily round to see what had interrupted its scratching.

A brown blob was hurtling up the slope below the cottage, faster than cloud-shadow. Love, freed from the leash of his training, was back now at the true centre of his nature, hunting. Love hunting Pibble.

The collie had raced to meet the intruder but was hoicked onto its hind legs by its lunge against the rope. Pibble began to lumber downhill, hoping to make it back to the half-safety of the collie's protection. A shadow moved in the doorway and the same brown arm that he had seen before reached out, but this time it didn't tug at the rope to quiet the collie. Instead steel gleamed for a moment in the bitter light.

The collie was loose, still yelping, stretching into a curving gallop with the slashed rope trailing behind it. Love never noticed this new enemy in his hurling across the wind-flattened grass. The collie was fresher, and perhaps

141

naturally faster. Pibble teetered to a halt – no point in running now, anywhere. Thirty yards from him the curved path intercepted the straight path, coming not quite at a tangent; as the dogs' shoulders met the collie's alligator jaw closed on Love's neck, but it was the surprise of the impact that bowled the bigger dog over, eight legs flailing as the collie clung to the brindled fur.

Love was up first. The fall had broken the collie's hold, and for a moment Pibble thought its back must be damaged as it threshed upside down in a patch of heather. Love shook his beautiful head and the tear behind his right ear showered a visible and arching spray of blood into the wind. Then he was leaping on, unbaffled.

But before he had made another five yards the collie was on him again and had bowled him over without letting go. As they flailed on the ground the long cord tangled round them. Mrs Macdonald was marching up the slope, her gutting knife held high above her head. She was yelling like a clansman. Far on the southern skyline a straggle of brown, skirted figures was beating through the heather. Pibble turned again and wallowed up the headland.

Ten minutes ahead of them, say; and there'd be a coracle for getting them to the boat, built for two at a pinch, and he'd be faced with one of those instant-logic problems – cannibals and missionaries crossing a river – one drunk, one loony, and one dotard, and poor old Pibble to ferry them over the water. Take Rita first, to climb into the boat. Then Sir Francis, and she could help him up. Wrestle with Dorothy last, if the monks hadn't come by then. They . . .

It turned out to be a big inflatable rubber dinghy, of the kind used for air-sea rescue. Rita had dragged it down into the water. As Pibble came swaying down the path, his hurt hip feeling as if there were lumps of gravel between bone and bone and his bruised feet slipping sockless in the unfamiliar boots, she was handing the old man over the rounded gunwale as though he were squiring her into a cotillon. By the time Pibble reached the weedy shore Sir Francis was grinning in the stern while Rita stood beside the foot-high wavelets, the diminished wind of the inlet swirling her habit about her in Diana-of-the-Uplands folds.

'Think you've got the whole damned afternoon to loiter about?' yelled the old man.

'She wasn't easy to lift,' said Pibble. 'The Virtues are coming up this way.'

'Maybe, maybe. Shake a leg, man. I'll be done for if I catch cold.'

Secondary infection, yes. Dangerous, the book had said. Pibble knelt on the slimy rock beside the gunwale with his hip as close to it as he could manage. Carefully he let himself keel over towards it, then at the edge of his balance he twitched and ducked under his own right hand which still held Sister Dorothy's wrist; as she toppled, he heaved shoreward. The twist and heave were agony, but her weight slid over the gunwale into the rocking dinghy. For a moment he felt so light that the wind could have blown him away. He lowered her on to her back, picked up her ankles and tucked them brutally in. Her interrupted snoring settled at once to a steady rasp.

'Get into the bows now, Countess,' he said. 'Sit a little over on the far side, and we'll be level again.'

She stepped daintily in. Pibble followed. Two rubber rowlocks projected from the fat gunwales, and when he fitted the stubby and splintery oars into them Pibble found that Dorothy's body was so disposed that it lay right across the place where he had to sit and row. He let go of the oars and wrestled with its inertness.

'Sit on her, you idiot!' shouted the old man. 'Row! She's used to it, hey? This thing's only made of rubber!'

Pibble looked up. The wind had already nudged the dinghy round and was drifting it down towards a reef of puncturing rocks at the bottom of the inlet. He settled into Sister Dorothy's lap with barely a twinge and started to pull with short strokes, lifting the oars high above the jerky wavelets each time he came forward. The toothed rocks receded, but still the funnelled wind shoved the dinghy crabwise. His right hand insisted on pulling more strongly than his left.

Sir Francis raised his walking-stick and for an instant Pibble thought the old man was going to strike him, but the ebony rod wavered and steadied to point over his right shoulder. Pibble pulled three times on his left oar and the pointer swung round, lifting over his head. Thus guided, he struggled with the sea.

Father had liked rowing. There'd been sweltering Sundays at Richmond, Mother in her wide hat, Father stripped to his waistcoat (he'd never have been seen in braces) and sporting a straw boater with a curiously broad ribbon, and small Jamie headachy from the sunbeams bouncing off the greasy water. Father, careful of his ruined lungs, had rowed with tidy economy, feathering, pocking the stream with regular little whirlpools where his oars had dipped; sometimes a passing boatload of oafs would mock raucously at his daintiness and Mother would flush, but he would row on unsweating, faster than many a splashing heaver. The cushions were brown, buttoned, sun-faded velvet; the seat-back varnished wicker. And once, when the day had soured into a squally wind and thunderclouds, they had hurried back from their picnic over a Thames that had real waves on it, all of six inches high. Then Father, explaining as usual, had rowed with an almost circular stroke, not feathering at all but lunging briefly at the water when the oars bit. That, he said, was how seamen managed waves. And he'd got Mother's new print dress back to the quay almost unspotted, while the boatloads of oafs cursed each other at every drenching stroke.

It worked, too, in a real sea with real waves. Pibble tugged steadily and Sir Francis never cursed him once.

The ebony stick speared skywards. Pibble eased, looked over his shoulder, tugged twice with his right oar and put up his hand to clutch the gunwale of the boat.

'You first,' yelled Sir Francis. 'You'll have to haul me up. Then the loony. Then you can come back for Dorrie.'

Pibble stood unsteadily and scrambled aboard. The un-decked half of the ship was a wild tangle of rotting fishing gear, nets and ropes rising into a herring-smelling mound under which the loose water in the bottom of the boat slopped soupily, rocked by his arrival. He found a loop of rope and hung it over the side, coiling the other ends round a T-shaped bit of brass made for some such purpose. He took the parcel which the mittened claws were waving at

144

him and found a nook for it on the netting.

'Put your foot in the loop, sir,' he said.

Sir Francis reversed his walking-stick and hooked it over the gunwale; carefully he pulled himself up; Pibble took his hands; Rita's slim arm, rough with gooseflesh, held the dinghy tight against the boat while Sir Francis pawed with his spatless foot and found the loop.

'Now!' said Pibble.

He was so light with age that Pibble almost tossed him against the far bulwark. They clutched each other like drunken waltzers but stayed upright. Sir Francis was already glaring round the boat.

'Damned Celts!' he said. 'Couldn't keep a shoe-box tidy! Bad as niggers – natives are always the same, wherever you go. Tie the painter and get the loony aboard. Tell her to find a place for me to nest while I see what sort of a mess those damned women have made of the rigging. You can heave Dorrie up.'

Pibble ran to the side and gave Rita her orders in his best Regency. He was worried about the time that had flickered by since Sir Francis had come to in the bothie. Rita had found the food-sack and was gnawing a corner of the loaf and looking as cold as a waif in a Christmas weepie, but she nodded and scrambled up. Pibble tied the painter and tumbled down to the heaving rubber. As soon as he knelt beside the snoring mass he knew that the job was beyond him. He was too weak to lift her now – he'd been too weak on firm land, dammit, and on this bulging and erratic platform . . .

He looked despairingly up. A shape on the shore nicked the edge of his eyesight. Lord Ullen's daughter poised by the sea-waves. No, it was Hope, the brown skirt of his habit stiff in the wind. Two others were at the cliff-top. Pibble stood and shouted to Sir Francis and pointed. The old man sneered at him.

'Can't reach us here, hey?' he said and returned to poking with his stick at the hummocks of red-brown cloth which lay beside the mast.

'I can't lift Sister Dorothy,' called Pibble. 'Can we tow her?'

'If you want to drown a good witness,' snarled Sir Francis. 'Wake the bitch up. Pour some water on her.'

Pibble knelt again, scooped the icy water in cupped hands and tossed it against the lined brown and open mouth. His victim shook her head and spat in her sleep. He tried again. This time she sat violently up, looked round the bay with eyes that seemed all rolling and bloodshot white, heaved herself to the gunwale and vomited. Pibble grabbed her by the shoulder as she was settling back to her stupor.

'Get aboard!' he shouted. 'We're going!'

He helped her to her knees, guided her hands to the gunwale of the boat, held the dinghy close in while he forced her into a crouch with his spare hand, got his shoulder under her buttock as she began to tumble, and heaved her inboard. He was afraid she might have broken her neck, but when he clambered up from the wallowing dinghy she was kneeling on the mount of netting, swaying like a slowing top.

'Bloody boats!' she said thickly and collapsed face down; her snore rose clear above the rattle of wavelets and the hissing wind and the endless, inane excitement of the wheeling gulls. Pibble lurched forward to where Sir Francis was still sitting by the hummock of sail, poking it with his stick.

Poking it without meaning or interest. He had gone soft.

'We're ready to go now, sir,' said Pibble.

'Well, get on with it, you damned fellow.'

'I need your help, sir.'

'Leave me alone. Can't you see I'm tired?'

Pibble looked up. Three Virtues now stood on the shore, and Providence was coming ponderously down the cliff path.

'Come back in three hours twenty minutes,' said the leaden voice. 'Where's Dorrie?'

Rita answered.

'She sleeps, Sire. But I am here, and your cabin is prepared. Here are your matches.'

Sir Francis put the little box away like an automaton and tried to rise. Rita helped him up.

'Stop!' said Pibble. 'I don't know how to sail the boat or

where to go.'

'Come back later,' mumbled the old man.

'His Majesty's command,' said Rita, 'is absolute law to all his subjects. Even the highest, Your Highness.'

'Reet,' said Pibble, 'the stones are your brothers.'

She laughed.

'Can you number the hairs of your own head, Reet?'

'Only . . . only . . .'

Her voice was changing. She stared wild-eyed round the incomprehensible sea-scape. Pibble toiled brutally on.

'Can you number the sins of your own heart, Reet?'

'Only God can number the sins of His own heart. And He has none.'

'And He has none. Go to the lonely cell, Reet, and wait for the word of the Lord to be made plain.'

He pointed to the low door. She shuffled in, dead-faced. Pibble took Sir Francis by the wrists.

'Sit down, sir,' he said gently.

'Damned insolence,' grumbled the old man, but allowed himself to be lowered on to the netting. Pibble settled him against Sister Dorothy's vibrating torso and went after for the food-sack. Providence was on the shore now. Hope had stripped. As if at a signal all the Virtues knelt on the rocks, and Providence raised both arms. The wind was the wrong way for Pibble to hear the words of their commination. He picked the bottle out of the sack, turned and settled himself beside Sir Francis. No snarl came through the old lips as he worked the watch out of the waistcoat pocket, flipped its back open and tipped the last ration of cortisone out into his palm.

'You haven't taken your pill, you naughty boy,' he cooed.

'Yes I have.'

'No you haven't. Open your mouth.'

It worked. The tongue, grey as fungus, protruded between the tensed lips. Pibble popped the pill on it and it flicked in.

'Water,' said the dull voice plaintively.

Pibble held the bottle to his lips and tilted. Perhaps, he thought, the mild lacing of spirit in it would act as a disinfectant against any bugs in the boggy water. Sir Francis

147

swallowed once, half choked, sneezed, shook his head and managed to finish his swallow. The spattering explosion produced an uncannily powerful reek. Pibble smelt the bottle. Crippen, this was *neat* whisky.

He sat on the netting and waited. Nothing happened. Providence was standing again, pointing at the enemies of the Faith, crying no doubt that his prayers had been answered and Sir Francis's senility had been visited on him before he could escape. Despairingly Pibble remembered the effect of salt water on Sister Dorothy and picked up a battered saucepan from the rubbish in the boat.

It would be a grisly risk – if the old man caught cold – perhaps a light sprinkling, and then dry him off with one of his shawls . . . He leaned over the bulwark.

Something slammed agonisingly into his back, and he nearly lost the saucepan. Clutching it he began to turn, but the pain caught him again, on the shoulder this time. He ducked down and sideways, looking for his enemy. There stood Sir Francis, eyes popping with rage, walking-stick raised for another blow.

'You damned insolent pup!' he shouted. 'I'll have you cashiered for this!'

'I can't sail the boat!' Pibble shouted back.

'My saints, can't an old man have a moment's peace? Do I have to do everything for you, you cretin?'

Sir Francis lowered his stick and looked round the inlet, grunting when he saw the group of Virtues.

'I'll get you out of here,' he said. 'Fetch the loony. She can cut the anchor rope. I haven't got long.'

Rita was in the cabin, on her knees, praying under a scarlet riding-light which she'd hung from a hook in the main beam.

'Come, Countess,' said Pibble. 'We need your aid.'

'The stones are my brothers,' she said. 'I will cut my die.'

Pibble crouched in under the low roof and took her icy hand.

'Come,' he said. 'It is the King's command.'

'There is only one King,' she said in her Sister Rita voice, 'and He is waiting for us to build Him His city.'

148

'Reet,' said Pibble. 'It is time for you to kill a great snake.'

She looked up, nodded, and rose to a crouch under the low beams. He led her out, plucked one of the gutting-knives from where they had been stuck in the bulwark, took her up on to the foredeck and showed her the taut hawser which ran through the guides in the bows.

'Cut it when I call,' he said.

She crouched beside the straining hemp holding the knife like a dagger. Pibble realised he'd have to get the weapon away from her as soon as she'd done her job. He went down to the well behind the mast and found to his despair that Sir Francis was once again poking with his stick at a mound of russet canvas.

'Are you all right, sir?'

'Course I am, you damned ninny, but I won't be if you keep me hanging around much longer. There's a winch under there, with a ratchet; you hoist the sail with it. Run it up steadily. Stop if it gets caught in anything. See that the ratchet-lock is working, so that it doesn't fall down when you let go. Got that?'

'Yes, sir.'

Pibble pointed to the shore. Hope had vanished from the group of monks, but a rounded, dark object was bobbing in the water. A pink arm rose and clove towards the boat with a sturdy stroke. And again.

'My saints,' said Sir Francis, staring, 'will I ever get used to the idiocy of truly damned idiots? Let me get aft.'

He tottered off under his mound of shawls. Pibble clawed and kicked at the brown canvas until he had lugged it clear of a battered old brass winch with a crank-handle that fitted over a square-cut projection from the axle. He started to turn. The locking pin clicked over the cogs. Beside him the brown mound heaved and a long spar rose slowly, hung from four pulleyed ropes along its length. The canvas threshed to and fro in the wind with a fearsome cracking and thumping, but Sir Francis seemed unperturbed so he wound on. Suddenly the winch would turn no more. He looked up and saw that its front end was taut against the mast, held by a series of rings which his winding had pulled up the mast. The spar and the back end of the sail still slapped back and forth. Hope was barely thirty foot away in the water. Pibble ran aft.

'Right,' said Sir Francis. 'Hold the sail out as far as you can that side and tell that loony to cut the rope.'

'Kill that snake, Reet,' he shouted.

She laughed at him, delicately.

'Coupez, contesse,' he bawled.

At once the blade flashed down as though she were skewering Marat at his ablutions. Then she had to saw. There came a bang and a rattle, and a lurch that nearly tipped the leaning Pibble out of the boat. The wind seemed to drop and the sail moved away from his reach and hardened into a clean curve. They were moving. The hustling waves rattled on the hull with a different note; the shore rocks drifted backwards. Hope had already turned and was swimming back towards his fellows with the same unflurried stroke.

'Come here,' shouted the old man. 'I'm damned near done for.'

You could hear in his voice that it was true. Pibble crouched beside him.

'Steer with this,' said the old man, 'and manage the sail with this. Those hags have left it reefed for you. You'll be damned sea-sick, but tell yourself you're Will Pibble's son, hey, and stick it out. Take the tiller first.'

Pibble settled beside him, winching at the harshness of the thwart, and took the tiller; he was astonished by the muscular feel of the water.

'Shove it over, you ninny,' said Sir Francis. 'You've got to balance the damned sail. Now take these.'

'These' were two ropes which ran to the top and bottom of the sail. Pibble took them in his left hand. Sir Francis grunted and leaned forward over his stick, struggling to rise. He couldn't make it.

'You've spitchered me, you damned interfering ninny,' he said, snarling like a dying vixen.

Pibble looked up and refocused his gaze from the narrowing rocks of the inlet mouth to where Rita stood statuesque by the mast.

'Countess!' he called.

She came with the swoop of a gull.

'My father is ill,' he said. 'Pray take him to the cabin and try to make him warm. If he catches cold he will die, and then all will be lost.'

'Alas!' she cried, and took the old man's hand, heedless of the angle of the tiller and the ropes that governed the sail. Her efforts combined with a lurch of the boat to tilt him to his feet, but at the same time tangled the ropes half round the pair of them.

'Look out!' cried Pibble, and leaned round the swaying couple to try and pull the ropes clear of them on the other side. His movement altered the angle of the tiller, just as the struggles of Rita and Sir Francis altered the angle of the sail. The rocks at the edge of his vision seemed to be moving differently, and he looked up from the crazy tangle to see that the boat was now moving, slowly but deliberately, almost straight for the right-hand shore. He pushed the tiller away from him, furious with fright. Slowly the boat's nose began to come round, with the cumbrous turn of a dowager acknowledging a lowly acquaintance at a flower show. They weren't going to make it.

But they did, easily. The curve of their course sharpened as the boat regained speed, and now they were pattering along parallel to the rocks. Rita found a hand to lift the impeding ropes over Sir Francis's head, and the sail stopped its waffling and banged out to its proper position. Craning below the curve of the sail-foot Pibble watched the leeshore edge away.

'Prize nincompoop!' complained Sir Francis, not in his leaden voice but rambling and slurring his words like a drunk. 'Prize . . . your mum was half right . . . Peace, not Physics . . .'

'Come, Your Majesty,' simpered Rita. 'His Highness comes worthily of a race of heroes. But our first task is to see you to safety.'

The pop eyes looked at her.

'Giddap, then,' he said with sudden liveliness. 'If I'm going to drown I'll do it with a bit of young flesh in my hands.'

She smiled and manoeuvred him round. The four-legged bundle of tweed and shawl edged away without turning either of its two heads. Pibble had a sense of rushing inescapably on, such as motor-cyclists experience when they first learn to use their machine, though he could see from the backward march of the cliffs that the boat was barely moving at a walking pace. This sense of speed came partly from the waves in the inlet being so small and close together, but beyond the sheltered water he could see the real waves loitering past, menacing, like the louts from a protection racket looking over an amusement arcade.

The gut of the inlet was a fair-sized target, but he was unable to coax the boat to its centre. Though he could steer – point the bows, that is – at what looked like the safest passage, the wind shoved from the left all the time, nursing him towards the black implacable grinders. A single rock stood eight feet above the water just beyond the entrance, and as the full-scale waves met it they bloomed into white water-spouts. He was worrying which side of it he should try to pass when the first real wave picked the boat up and shook it like a dice in a gambler's paw. He only just stayed upright, bracing himself on the thwart.

Then came the full wind, tilting the mast so far over that the pitted hummocks on the black surface of the wave slid along the gunwale as if all the cold sea were going to pour in, but the boat stayed, poised at that angle, while the next wave shook them.

This time he fell; the ropes slid from his flailing hand; he pounced as the coil of rope in the bottom of the boat began to snake away, and hauled the sail back, then grabbed at the swinging tiller. Gasping, he looked about him.

The mast stood more upright now that the sail was eased. But the boat was heading straight for the spouting rock. Gulping he shoved the tiller the other way. The bows nosed, like a dog smelling a stranger's hand, at the limpet-deckled surface and swung suspiciously away. But the passing wave seemed to suck them back and down; a low, drum-like, rasping boom shook the whole boat, and its live movement in the water deadened at the stone touch. They slid along the granite upright, still turning away – as a dog, suspicions allayed, might rub against the stranger's shins. Something checked the sliding for a moment, and the rasping dulled. With a mild explosion the forgotten dinghy shredded on its tether.

Then the next wave was on them, flipping them out again, yards from the deadly menhir; just as Pibble was releasing the pent air from his lungs the spume of spouted water stung down on him. He staggered, as though the ocean had crept up behind him and coshed him with a salt-water club. He shook his head; they'd only shipped a bucketful but Dorothy had received a salt-water slap in the face and was frowning in her stupor. The boat seemed to be sailing reasonably straight, on a course that would soon take them clear of the island to a point where he might be able to spot the lighthouse, the first sea mark on their journey home. Once there, Sir Francis should have come round again. He knew these seas. Pibble's task now was to learn how to reconcile this single-minded wind with the quaquaversal water.

In the trough between the waves the gunwales lay lower than the marching crests; he felt like the mayor of a village beneath a crumbling dam. Then the boat would sidle, untold, up the slope of another menace and there he'd teeter, poised above a tilted world, dizzy as a child tossed to the ceiling by a raucous godfather. But after a while he decided that nothing would go wrong if he kept to this course, the boat, in its lumpish way, seemed to know what it was doing. He looked southeast, over his right shoulder.

From the ridge of the first wave he saw nothing but whirling sea beneath unrelated sky; on the second he located the blurred horizon; soon he was orientated enough to start searching the line of it – and there, as though the pencil had slipped on the ruler, was a notch in its straightness. Nothing else could be Dubh Artach lighthouse. There lay his path, as soon as he was far enough north to be sure of clearing the island. He remembered from the map, and his peerings out of the helicopter, they'd have to make a huge dog-leg southeast, right round the lighthouse, to be sure of reaching the Firth of Lorne. Otherwise he'd be in danger of piling them up on the very rocks on which David Balfour was wrecked in *Kidnapped*.

Before trying to turn he glanced aft. Clumsey Island was a drab cliff half a mile back; the spouting rock made a white blink against the blackness of the headland. He put the ropes between his teeth, raised his left hand and waved Byronically.

Home James.

8

He failed to turn. Instead he nearly drowned them all.

Television and the Hornblower books had hitherto been his total knowledge of the sea, but even from them he knew that you couldn't just turn. You had to 'come about', wasn't it? Obviously, if you just pushed the rudder over there'd come a point when the wind got behind the sail and slammed it across hard enough to snap the mast. And there'd be no accounting for the manners of the waves while that was happening. What you did was to point the bows *towards* the wind, and get round that way.

Nudging the boat round came easily enough, though at the changed angle the waves sprayed high over the bows and stung like hailstones as the big drops hurtled aft. At each change of angle he hauled the sail in another few inches, so that it would have less far to travel when the moment came to turn. There came a point, down in a trough, when all seemed still and poised. He put the helm over.

It was a bad choice. As the sail lost its rigid curve and began to flail and flog, the boat nuzzled boldly into the oncoming wave, prodding its bows into the green meat of it. Instantly the whole top of the wave flowed in tearing foam across the upper deck and fell in a white cataract into the well. The boat jarred and faltered. Pibble shoved the tiller back to where it had been and watched, helpless with doom, while half a ton of water sluiced through the mound of netting and round his ankles. The sail hardened back into its old place. The boat raised its weary snout from the wallow. They were sailing again, but still north.

When Father was dead, Mother had insisted on dancing lessons, on the grounds that they would be 'useful'. Or perhaps it had been part of a vague campaign against Mr Toger's obliterating puritanism, forcing poor Jamie into Sunday trousers and Sunday shoes on a Saturday afternoon when he could have been up on the Common, and that special shirt with lacy cuffs, and sending him off to the upper room at the Pakenham Arms where Miss Fergusson, daughter of a bishop, held her class in an upstairs room. Four boys and a dozen girls. The girls danced happily with each other, bouncing through the waltzes, while the boys sulked by the wall. But then Miss Fergusson would look up from the piano, stop her shrill iteration of *one*twothree, and notice that she was cheating four sets of parents of their shilling-an-hour. Oh then began the torment of his soul. The girl would be bigger, know the steps; four or five bars together the dance would go right and then, inexplicably, an unwanted step would insert itself between the *one* and the two, and he'd be shuffling, lost, until the girl stopped, counted the steps for him with patient disdain, and re-started him for another five bars. And again. And again. Until Miss Fergusson's head was bent once more over the key-board, her heart waltzing with dead officers, and the girls could nod to each other, toss the boys back into hiding and dance off together.

The sea never stopped. It knew its own rhythm, and would sometimes let Pibble into the secret for five loping waves, but then with a lurch and stagger he'd lose the beat and the boat would fumble awkwardly from trough to trough. A particularly bad lurch came as he was trying to nerve himself to the responsibility of continuing north to Tiree in the hope of finding a telephone at midnight and sending for help. If they went much further, Oban would be out of reach. And what would the old man say? Poor old Pibble. Perhaps it would be better to try and turn again . . .

The boat swooped and then staggered, tumbling Dorothy clean off her hill of netting into the water that sloshed along the planking. For an instant she lay face down, then jerked herself on to hands and knees with a raucous snort and glared at Pibble.

'What the bloody hell are you playing at?' she said.

'I'm sorry,' said Pibble. 'There's some dry clothes in the cabin.'

She crawled forward into the dark cavern. She seemed a long time gone, but when she came out she was wearing a jersey and trousers and carrying oilskins.

'You'll need this,' she said sourly, passing one to him. 'What's that bloody little whore doing with Frank?'

'She's a schizophrenic,' snapped Pibble.

'She's two bloody little whores, then.'

'We wouldn't have got this far without her.'

'Keep calm. I was a bloody little whore myself, once. Where are we, for Christ's sake?'

'We're trying to go over there,' said Pibble, 'but I don't know how to turn the boat. I shipped a lot of water last time I tried, so I didn't dare do it again.'

'Well, that's one comfort. I thought the bloody boat was leaking. I'll turn her while you bail. Christ, I could do with a drink.'

'There *is* a bottle of whisky,' said Pibble doubtfully. 'But it would be a great help if you contrived to remain . . . er . . .'

'Oh, God!' she said. 'Here we go again. If it isn't bloody old Frank who needs me, it's a bloody little copper whose name I've forgotten.'

'Pibble.'

'All right, Mr Pibble, I'll stay this side of swine-drunk.'

Pibble picked up the bottle from under the thwart and handed it to her. She took a healthy swig. And another. He put the ropes between his teeth to snatch it away, but at that moment she lowered it and corked it up.

'That's more like it,' she said. 'Right. Give me the tiller.'

At once the prancing of the boat eased. Dorothy sniffed the wind, looked at the sail, fiddled with the ropes, said 'lee-oh', and quite lackadaisically put the helm over. The boat came up into the wind, and a nicely-judged wave twitched it further. The sail flapped across, everything tilted the other way, Dorothy let the sail out and fastened the ropes, which Pibble had been so anxiously clutching, round a cleat, and there they were, sailing southeast.

'Can you see the lighthouse?' said Pibble.

'Yup. Nip off and see that Frank and the little bint are OK. Then you'd better come back and bail.'

It was more like a kennel than a cabin; its beams were barely three feet above its floorboards; from one of them hung a red riding-light, by whose nasty glow he could see an inch of water slopping in the down-hill corner, its ripples red-ridged in the red light. Rita and Sir Francis were propped on a pile of canvas right up in the far corner, where the bows came together. Sir Francis had all the spare clothes draped about him up to his scrawny neck, so that his head protruded from undecipherable parts of trousers and jerseys. It may have been the light, but Pibble thought he saw a different look on the antique features from any he'd yet seen there – less bleak, less fierce, no less selfish. And not all the gurgles came from slopping water; Sir Francis's lips and gullet were making some of them.

And Rita, smiling her sweet, demented smile, hugged close against him, as close as Love had nuzzled to Pibble on the quay. She was breathing in huge gasps – no, it was the mittened claw moving in scaly caresses under her jersey.

'They look all right,' reported Pibble.

'You've got to admire the old bastard, haven't you? There'll be a loose board under the water there, and you can bail with that saucepan. They won't have a proper pump on a bloody old tub like this.'

She was right about the board. Pibble crouched stiffly and began to scoop in the extra depth made by its removal.

'You're not much of a hand in boats,' she said.

'I've never tried before. Sir Francis, er, lost hold before we got the sail up, but I managed to wake him up enough to get us out of the inlet.'

'Bloody hell! How did you manage that?'

'I gave him another of his pills.'

'That wouldn't do it.'

'I washed it down with neat whisky in mistake for water.' Dorothy cackled.

'That might,' she said. 'A bloody great physical outrage. How did he take it?'

'He hit me with his walking-stick.'

'I bet he did. He's not used to that sort of handling.'

'He's got Addison's Disease, hasn't he?' said Pibble.

'Yes.'

'I read about it in a book in Brother Patience's room. It didn't say anything about, er, periods of inattention.'

'Do you know a lot of old people, Mr Pibble?'

'Not as old as him. My family tend to die younger.'

All two of them. Scoop, scrape, toss, scoop . . . something seemed to have diluted the acid in her voice a degree or so . . . three gallons a minute, say, that's thirty pounds. A ton of water would take . . .

'They hate it,' she said. 'Being old, I mean. Even if they're sweet old ladies, they hate being dependent, they hate being tired, they hate being stupid. And they've got to be all three, most of the time. Frank's Frank, and he's coped his own way. When he's on the spot, he's all there, just as bloody as ever. When he's not, he's gaga. It's his way of eating his cake and having it. He's too stuck-up to be half-clever, or half-bloody, so when he's not up to it he resigns. The world isn't there at all, as far as he's concerned, except to cosset him until he comes to and takes charge again.'

'I thought the four-hour cycle was too handy to be natural.'

'Oh, it's natural *now*. But he started it off like that quite deliberately, so that poor bitches like me would be waiting at his door, ready to crawl for him the moment he came to. Four goes into twenty-four, so it's the same bloody moment six times each day.'

'How long have you known him?'

'Thirty-three and a quarter years. Since I was nineteen. I took over from a jealous old hag of twenty-eight, and nobody took over from me. Where's that bottle?'

She took another long swig and handed it to him.

'Have a go yourself,' she said. 'I wouldn't be so crazy sick for the stuff if I had someone human to talk to. Twenty years it's been since I could nip round somewhere and have a chin-wag with a crony. And it's been worse since we came to this bloody place.'

'Why did you come?' said Pibble, probing one mystery.

'Search me,' she answered. 'We were damned poor, of course. Frank gave all his money away, except for a few copyrights on books, when he set up his Foundation, and he hadn't got out of the habit of spending. *He* wasn't going to ask for charity, either. We'd been up on this coast a couple of times before that, doing a bit of sailing, rummaging about like a dog which can't find a bone it's buried; but there were always reporters with their little notebooks and hotel managers fawning and charging us double, and we bolted back to London. Then he had his op; then he gave all the cash away, and all his radio patents and shares, to set up his Foundation; then he got the Peace Prize and we lived on that for a few years. And then, when we were down to our last thousand quid, though there was still a little dough coming in from books and pamphlets, I was washing his feet one morning and he said "Ring up Carter Paterson – we're going to live on Clumsey Island". 'We left next week.'

'That must have been a shock for you.'

'It was bloody, but I'd got used to the world being bloody by then.'

'When you talk about a little money, coming in from books and pamphlets, how much do you mean?'

'Two or three thousand a year. I've never known a man grudge his taxes like Frank did.'

'Yes, I know,' said Pibble. 'He told me . . . oh, Crippen, what a fool I am!'

'No more than the rest of us. You mustn't let him get you down.'

'I didn't mean that. He came here because it's a charity under the Charities Acts. He made over his copyrights to them, and they don't pay tax. Then when he wanted to write a really lucrative book he didn't fancy their getting all the money. He knew they wouldn't want to let him go, so he sent for me. But meanwhile they'd copied the book and sold it in London, which they'd managed to do because they'd already been dealing in his name with agents and publishers over the other books. It only needed a few forged signatures. Then when I turned up, they knew we'd talk about the book, so they decided to kill him by taking away his pills.'

'What the bloody hell are you talking about?'

Pibble explained it all as Clumsey Island rose larger and nearer on the starboard bow.

'Christ!' she said. 'I told you they were bastards.'

'One thing you haven't told me,' said Pibble, 'is why he gave his money away in the first place.'

'He never told *me*,' she said. 'But I think I've worked it out. He was always funny about money. He was bloody rich but he didn't behave as if it mattered. It was just stuff he happened to have the use of, but he wasn't stuck-up about it, like most rich men are. It was just money he'd sort of *found*, under a stone or somewhere. I'm not saying he was generous, mind you – he was mean. Then he had his op, and after that this disease got him and he was frightened. That was nearly ten years ago. He thought he was dying, and he wanted to take his revenge on the world before he died.'

'Revenge for what?'

'Everything. Look, Mr Pibble, you must sometimes wake up in the night and curse yourself for the things you've done and curse the world for the things it's done to you. You rail at bits of your fate, then, but not at all of it, and not all the time. Frank rails at the whole thing. Everything that's ever happened to him has been unfair. He was dealt this colossal hand and then God cheated him. *My* life's been bloody, maybe, but it hasn't been unfair. Frank's has, he thinks – every second of all those years.'

Pibble was silent, baling. Scoop, scrape, toss.

'The doctors gave him about six years,' said Dorothy. 'They were guessing, of course, and worse than usual because no one's ever had Addison's Disease as old as Frank. So he set up the Foundation, partly because it meant that he dictated what happened to the money, but mainly to get the Peace Prize. He worked like a black for that, you know. He nosed about and decided exactly what would catch the jury's fancy, and set up the Foundation as bait; and he started being nice to journalists and being saintly and forbearing in public – I expect it's all in his book, how he pulled a confidence trick on the Establishment. And he'll lash out at Einstein – he always hated him – and he'll say what a frightful thing peace is, and how war brings the right men to the top and kills off the nuisances . . .'

'That's another reason why he had to escape,' said Pibble.

'I don't see it.'

'They'd never have printed that sort of stuff once he was dead.'

'Why did he choose you?'

'He saw my name in a newspaper cutting. My father worked for him before the First World War.'

'That's a funny reason for trusting you. Frank doesn't usually trust anybody.'

'He didn't trust me. He sent Providence a sealed envelope – you gave it back to me – in case I tried to exploit him in some way. Providence must have opened the seal, because he accused me of rushing up here to make a mysterious claim on Sir Francis's estate, and Sir Francis himself asked me whether my father ever said anything about the fact that he ought to have been damned rich. There was a legend in my family that Sir Francis had stolen something from my father, but not money, just an idea.'

'That's bloody peculiar,' said Dorothy. 'I've known him a long time. First he was just himself, working like a digger in a mine disaster. Sometimes he'd surface for a few days of crazy fun, like a sailor on leave from the North Sea convoys, but mostly he wouldn't say a word for weeks on end, not even a thank you, not even in bed. He'd just hurtle on. I *knew* him then, of course, but I didn't know much *about* him. After the war – he loved the war – he got older and slower. That's when he started to talk so much – it's a defence against having to listen at all to the rest of us idiots. And it was mostly me he talked to, because he hadn't any real work. He'd still a lot of work in him, but he couldn't find a set-up that would have him because everyone knew what a bastard he was to have about the place. Even Berkeley wouldn't find a job for him.'

'Wasn't he rich enough to set up his own establishment?' said Pibble, switching the saucepan to his left hand and hunkering round to a new pose. Perhaps the water-level was half an inch lower.

'Christ!' said Dorothy. 'You don't know what Frank's sort of toy costs these days. You make a vacuum, you start a sort of atomic explosion in it, and you try to control it with magnetic fields. It's mostly maths, but then you've got to build the bloody thing and see if it works. They haven't so far, and of course Frank says that because they wouldn't ask *him*. But supposing some maniac stood him the equipment, even then he could only just afford the running costs, and he was a millionaire twice over. That was what I was coming to. He talked a lot, and he didn't repeat himself as much as old men usually do, but I don't think he ever said anything about where the first big dollop of money came from. I know he was poor at Cambridge and rich after the war, and I remember a Buckingham Palace Garden Party where he teased a nice old general by telling him that he'd had the sense to be a war profiteer while the stupid ones were dying in the mud – What's up?'

'I'm going to be sick,' said Pibble, and was, so far as his stomach would supply him with vomit.

'Nothing you can do about it,' said Dorothy, with neither pity nor contempt when at last he pushed himself up, icy with feverish sweat, from the wet gunwale and the black-green, puckered, bubbling, backward-streaming sea.

'By the time I knew him,' she said, 'he had his money tied up in a tangle of radio patents and directorships of radio companies. He made a packet out of the second war, too. Christ, I won't be sorry if I never see that place again.'

She nodded towards the west, up the hill of the leaning boat. Pibble knelt on the netting and looked; they were now re-passing the shambling wedge of Clumsey Island, with the buildings projecting towards the thinner end. The imprecision of the verticals combined with the lumpiness of the design to make the place look like an unnatural growth – up-thrusting from the sour earth, all scaly where the light gleamed from the slates. Pibble stared at the place, unable even to summon up the aesthetic energy to dismiss it as ugly.

From the growth an insect rose and hung, a spiky black blob, to the left of the tower. Pibble's instant panic lasted only its instant. Hope must be flying the helicopter, perhaps taking Tolerance to the mainland for hospital treatment. Providence would be with him, certainly. They would go to Oban, rout the authorities out, tell them – holy and solemn – that a demented policeman had invaded the island, kidnapped the great Sir Francis and two nuns, and had also caused Grievous Bodily Harm to one inoffensive anchorite, beside extensive damage to property.

Would it work? The GBH was nasty; Pibble's mythical claim on the old man's estate might be worked up into a madman's motive; Rita and Dorrie were useless witnesses, for either side. But Sir Francis, when compos, should be a match for the lot of them. Suppose, though, that the boat came to Oban in one of his senile patches . . . then they'd try to toddle the old man off and keep him out of the way of help until the lack of cortisone had crumbled his mind. But once Pibble could reach a policeman, a telephone, his own context, he'd be able to . . . But Providence would realise that. They'd try to stop him getting there; hire a launch in Oban, board the boat in the dark. That could work, but . . .

'They can't get at us here, can they?' said Dorothy.

'I don't think they want to,' said Pibble. 'They're making for Oban.'

'You can't tell *what* the bastards want,' she said.

The drup of rotors reached him down the wind. The helicopter was going to pass very near – it could fly straight to Oban while the boat had to take the long dog-leg round Dubh Artach lighthouse. Ironic if it passed straight over them – no, it would come about fifty yards behind. He could see the two cowled heads, dim behind the crazed perspex of the cabin-bubble, but couldn't distinguish which Virtues they belonged to. One was moving about, tugging at something – the door!

A new panic sluiced through him as the ugly machine, erratic in the wind, swung round over the equally erratic wake which Dorothy had steered. It thudded towards them. Hope would hand over the controls, slide like a gymnast down a rope, prance on to the deck and break him apart, sad but ruthless.

'Can you go more down-wind?' he shouted.

164

The boat lurched round. Even Pibble knew (from a dismal three days spent raking Cobham Moor for a vanished school-girl, himself directing the soaked lines of searchers from on high by walkie-talkie) that it is hard for a helicopter to hover downwind. Either they hadn't brought Tolerance or he'd fainted, for he'd have told them that.

'Get a knife!' screamed Dorothy. 'There's one in the gunwale!'

He ran to where the second gutting-knife projected from the scarred wood. The only chance was to catch the ruffian saint at the one vulnerable moment when he landed. He climbed up to the foredeck, so as to have the upper ground. Dorothy shouted something, but her voice was drowned by the drubbing rotors. The sail flapped and loosened in the downdraft, and the boat suddenly lost way. The machine was beyond the mast and rocking as though its crew were wrestling together.

One of them had fallen out!

The black mass, too small and compact for a tumbling body, hurtled down to vanish in a waterspout ten feet beyond the bows. Only as the splash resettled did Pibble see, on his retina's memory, what had actually fallen. A boulder. Two hundredweight of murderous rock. A stone bomb. The Community was going to solve the Pibble question after the fashion of the Eternal City.

He watched dully as the helicopter circled to line itself up again. This time they would have had some target-practice. They would drop their stone bomb sooner.

'What happened?' yelled Dorothy.

'They tried to drop a rock on us, but the downdraft from the rotors slowed us down and they overshot. They're going to try again.'

Dorothy began to curse. Though her words were an ordinary string of ordinary foulnesses she spoke them like a hag calling powers from the pit.

'Can you try and dodge?' he said.

The boat, hitherto a tiny fleck on the enormous sea, refocused under the lens of terror to a spreading, unmissable target.

'Or if there's a way of stopping the boat before they reach

165

the sail,' he said, 'they might overshoot again.'

'Oh Christ!' she said. 'You can try it. Get the pawl off the ratchet and hold it with the handle. The gaff will bring the sail down when you let go, and we'll stop pretty nearly dead.'

Pibble ran to the winch, wrenched the handle round so that he could flick the pawl out of the cogs, and knelt to watch the enemy. This time the helicopter seemed to be coming slower; now he was sure that the one at the controls was Hope. A pale round bulge protruded at the side of the bubble, Providence's head; beyond it beard flapped like a college scarf. When the helicopter was six feet astern he shouted to Dorothy. She put the tiller over.

Too soon. The machine overshot as the boat swung soggily left, but didn't drop its missile. It came round in a tight circle and was six feet behind again. He shouted again; a splodge of wave-top caught the back of his neck as the boat plunged right and the sail rattled loose. Dorothy hauled it in, but this time Hope hadn't needed to circle but had followed them round. The roaring contraption wobbled as Providence tussled with another boulder. Only seconds to go now. Pibble saw its jagged side, shouted, and jerked the handle off the winch.

The sail knocked him flat beneath its banging folds. He felt the boat plunge and wallow, a toy of the sea. He got his head out from the canvas and saw the helicopter, toy of the wind, flick forward. The boulder was over the sill; a hand was clawing at it, trying to haul it back; if that hand had shoved, it would have fallen on the bows; but the hand was not strong enough; the stone edged outwards, slow as molasses beginning to drip from the edge of a spoon; now it was falling like the first.

The waterspout was nearer this time. Because the boat was no longer moving with the wind he could see, as he struggled to his feet, the circular swirl where the stone had fallen heave up by the bows and then vanish as the next wave tilted the wallowing vessel back.

'Get the bloody sail up!' shouted Dorothy.

He kicked and hustled the canvas clear of the winch, found the handle and started to wind, battered by the iron-hard folds, which flapped back and forth. When it was taut he ran aft to where Dorothy was trying to hold the sail-foot out to her left with one hand and control the tiller with the other.

'I'll do the sail,' he gasped, took the corner of canvas from her and leaned as far out as he dared. A hand grabbed at his waistband and hard knuckles dug into his spine. He leaned further, and the canvas hardened to a curve – on the wrong side of the boat. Ah, yes, that was the only way to pull the bows round, out of the wind. He leaned and strained. A wave creamed along the gunwale and slopped into the well.

'Right,' said Dorothy.

He let the sail go. It smacked to its proper place. The boat was moving properly through the water again.

He looked wildly round for the helicopter. It was going away, back to Clumsey Island.

'Think the bastards will try again?' said Dorothy.

'They'll have to, now,' said Pibble, watching the spindly blob diminish, low over the waves.

'What the bloody hell do they think they're up to?' said Dorothy.

'They want Sir Francis dead, and me too. They don't think you and Rita matter, either way. I'll try to rig some nets. There might be a signal rocket. If we can get near enough to the lighthouse for the crew to see us, they won't risk dropping rocks on us.'

'Bloody sea,' said Dorothy. 'Bloody boats. I always hated them, but Frank made me learn. We won't be any-where near the lighthouse before they get back. Isn't there a lifeboat in this stinking tub?'

'It burst on a rock,' said Pibble. 'What do you think about rigging nets?'

'You'd never get the bloody things up in time. What's that?'

Pibble knelt among the nets and scrabbled at a bundle half-buried beneath them. 'INFLATE' said the stencilled letters. He hauled out an awkward, rubbery parcel and found it was another Air-Sea Rescue dinghy – some fishing crony must have unloaded a batch of Government Surplus stores on the innocent Macdonalds. He tumbled it back against the bulwarks and turned for the cabin.

'Blow the bloody thing up!' shouted Dorothy behind him, her voice teetering above the cliffs of hysteria. He knelt, unlashed the fastenings, removed a yellow metal cylinder two feet long, and began to work the little hand-bellows. The dinghy puffed up a treat – why, if he could heave it about the boat fast enough it might cushion the first impact of a falling rock enough to save the underlying timbers. In that case he didn't want it blown up tight. As he puffed his eyes looked uncomprehendingly at the picture on the yellow cylinder, which showed a pilot sitting snugly in his dinghy and fiddling with a contraption of cloth and struts. There were instructions above the picture, but the curve of the cylinder only allowed him to read the last one:

6. TO HAUL IN KITE AFTER USE. WIND IN LINE AROUND THE CONTAINER TO PREVENT TANGLING.

He looked towards the island. It was small already. Soon it would be no more than a grey hummock. The sky above it was bare.

'Kite,' nudged the erratic remembrancer in the court of his skull. Yes, a pilot in a dinghy would fly one to attract attention. It would be bright-coloured, and far more visible than an object at sea-level. Perhaps the lighthouse crew might spot it – if he could get it to fly. Kites don't for Pibbles.

Inside the lid of the cylinder was a little yellow cardboard box, octagonal in section, containing (the instructions said) 33 yards of flying line. He tipped it out and peered at the besom-like cluster of aluminium twigs below. He could pull them as far as the end of the cylinder, where they jammed under the incurled rim. When he freed one, another jammed on the far side. With dismal patience he fiddled each twig free and withdrew the whole besom, whose further end was lapped in yellow cloth. **REMOVE RUBBER BANDS FROM FABRIC, ASSEMBLE THE FOUR MAIN LONGERONS BY INSERTING THE TUBE ENDS INTO THEIR CORRESPONDING HALVES.**

Now the toy was three feet long, four flimsy struts swathed at either end in yellow cloth whose flappings concealed another mess of metal twigs.

SHAKE KITE PARTIALLY OPEN. PRESS OUTWARDS ON THE SPIDERS AT EACH END UNTIL THE SPREADING MEMBERS SEAT IN THEIR OUTWARD POSITION. (see illustration)

And the thing was alive in his hands, a box kite, already nuzzling at the wind as a lap-dog strains against the leash at the entrance to the Park.

SHOULD THE WIND SPEED BE LESS THAN 20 MPH, THE FLYING LINE SNAP HOOK SHOULD BE LOWERED TO THE 'BOTTOM' BRIDLE POINT ON THE KITE – *THIS IS IMPORTANT*.

On the straining cloth the same peremptory slugs of jargon were printed, with further diagrams. Even a damned fool like your dad could fly *this* kite, provided he'd brought his anemometer along.

'How fast is the wind?' he yelled.

'Twenty knots, I'd say. What the hell are you playing at?'

'If I get this up the lighthouse might see it.'

'Not a hope. The cord might bother the bastards, like a barrage balloon.'

Um. Surely even Tolerance's dicey rotors would slice through that. It'd take wire . . .

He took the toy up to the foredeck, clipped the safety-pin-like shackle on the end of the flying line through the 20 mph loop, held the kite high and let go. It dithered for an instant in the lee of the sail; he gave it more line and it ducked, then soared. It went almost straight up as he let the cord gently out, but when he tried to hurry it by giving it slack it began to tumble like a shot pheasant. Two tugs and it was climbing again. He knotted the end of the cord to the bow stay wire and ran back to the well to search for something tough enough to smash a rotor. Or perhaps he could find a signal-rocket to shoot at them – though it would need a fluke on the verge of fantasy to hit such a target.

There was nothing useful among the netting, so he ducked into the cabin. Rita was asleep now, her head on the old man's shoulder and her long locks coiling among the bristling whiskers like clematis in a dead apple-tree. Sir Francis blinked at the swaying light and mumbled to himself. The water on the floor was almost gone – so his baling had had some effect. He hunted among the lockers.

There had been a signal-rocket, once, but something heavy and sharp had been dumped on it and now it gaped like a gutted fish; its powdery innards mottled the locker floor. Another locker held fishing-reels, weights and bait-tins; the next a tangle of blocks and cords, but nothing thin enough to fly a kite from. The boat gave a wild lurch and he stumbled to the floor. He snatched a coil of staywire from the locker and crawled out to see what had happened.

Dorothy was back at the tiller, but she must have left it for now she had the bottle to her lips, tilted like a trumpet. Pibble staggered across the netting and snatched it away, making a spout of pale amber spurt across her cheek. She grabbed at his arm but he held the bottle over the bulwark.

'I'll drop it,' he said.

She nodded, scooped her hand across her cheek and licked at her whisky-flavoured palm. Pibble found the cork at her feet, stoppered the bottle and put it under his arm. Far over Clumsey Island he could see a dark spot rising. The lighthouse seemed not an inch nearer than before.

'You're just as bloody a bastard as the rest of them,' she said thickly. 'If I'm going to die, why can't I die happy?'

The hair-of-the-dog sour reasonableness which her first swigs had given her was gone. Now she'd be drunk again. Already she was steering the boat with broad gestures which made it swoop and stumble.

He settled the bottle into a coil of rope on the foredeck, then tugged at the kite-string while he poised the coil of wire in his other hand and tried to guess what the kite would lift, a job as hopelessly chancy as estimating the raisins in a cake at one of Mary's charity fetes. About half the wire, maybe. He knelt on the deck to measure out the springy and self-tangling stuff, looped it, scuttered down to the well for the wind-handle, held the loop over the iron anchor-guide in the bows, and hammered at the wire with the handle. The loop wouldn't stay vertical, and the doubled wire pinched at his left palm. He caught it a lucky wallop which bent it to a proper kink that he could really hit. As he hammered, a croaking yell came through the deck beneath him – serve the old scorpion right. He bent the kink back on itself and hammered with fresh strength. Wristily he waggled the wire on either side of the battered kink to and fro. His thumbs scorched with the abrasion of rough strands. At the kink, all at once, two strands changed colour to a whitish grey, and fractured. Then another. He hammered again at the remaining strands, waggled again, reduced the kink to two obstinate strands which broke after the next hammering. He looked over his shoulder.

The helicopter was a spiky blob now – four minutes away, maybe. As he was lashing the kite-string to the wire he had a better idea. He looped the wire round a cleat and ran to the cabin. Sir Francis called him a damned fellow. He tried the fishing reels. One large one ran smoothly and held a fat line which he couldn't break with all his strength; flicking its brass catch to and fro he darted back – one position to wind, one to aft, one to let free. He tied the fishing line to the kite-string so that the wire would dangle loose and paid out wire and line together. The kite rose, seeming to get no smaller, taking the extra weight without wavering; down the taut line he could feel the muscles of the wind. The end of the wire came in a desperately short time, and he let it fall clear. Above the wind and waves he heard the sullen thud of the rotors. He still had to get aft, to bring the wire as near as he could to the boat's centre.

But no, the machine was flying parallel to their course, about a hundred yards away, its tail tilted cockily up behind the gawky cabin where the two holy murderers crouched black against the evening sky. They must be puzzling out the meaning of his toy – perhaps, through the blurring perspex, they wouldn't see the wire.

Not thinking what he was doing, hypnotised by the bumbling menace, Pibble wound out more line.

The helicopter swung round across their path, three hundred yards ahead, swung further, lined itself up, and came towards them. The monks had discovered the error of attacking down-wind. Pibble shouted to Dorothy and pointed down the line of the kite. She shouted back, put the tiller over, loosed the sail a few degrees, and they were plunging straight down-wind towards the pitiful protection of the staywire – and even that twenty-foot thread of steel was shortened by the curves left in it from the coil. If it had weighed less it would have dangled almost over the bows; but as it was, Hope could dodge round it and come in behind.

The helicopter had paused in mid-air and edged sideways, into their new path. A hundred yards. It rocked as its load was trundled towards the door. Get aft, you fool, and the wire will be twenty foot nearer the boat.

No, wait. They were coming in very low this time. They had seen the wire, and for fear of being dodged were coming not round, but under. Desperately he began to wind the fishing line in. There wasn't time.

He pressed the brass catch that let the reel fly.

The kite swooped out and down, tumbling dead from the sky, like any kite he'd ever owned. The wire rushed out and down, too. The helicopter, its reactions as slow as an old bruiser's, tilted late to the left. The kite was still tumbling, then it steadied and jerked up as though something had dragged for an instant at its line, and then it was tumbling again.

And so was the helicopter. A biggish morsel of rotor curled away. The machine staggered and rocked, rocked so wildly that the poised boulder spilt and hurtled to the waves – bigger than the last two, a real megastone. Freed of the weight of it the helicopter tumbled more slowly down, its unbalanced rotor threshing.

'Steer as close to them as you can!' shouted Pibble as he stumbled aft and started to heave at the ungraspable edges of the dinghy. He got one side of it over the bulwark by hauling, wriggled round and shoved from the other side until he had it poised.

The helicopter's cabin was still above the water as the boat surged up; the rotor had stopped, but the tail was sinking and the weight of the rotor-shaft was tilting the structure sideways when Pibble shoved at the dinghy. He was too weak now to do more than slop it over the side, but a wave cradled it and then slid it across the ten-foot gap so that it bobbed close alongside the tilting cabin.

Providence was on his feet, shouting, his hand at the door-rim, his cheeks and forehead purple. From beyond him a brown sleeve snaked up, caught him by the neck, dragged him back to his seat and held him there. He went on shouting, but Hope, sitting brotherly beside him with a face as impassive as a seraph's, locked him to the seat as the next wave rolled the machine slowly over and the downward drag of the tail tilted its nose towards the sky.

Another wave smashed across it in spume, as if hitting a sunken rock, and when the pother cleared the helicopter was gone. If a bubble rose, it did so out of sight.

The rubber dinghy lolloped into view and out again, a slow pulse on the skin of the sea. Dorothy stopped singing 'For he's a jolly good fellow.'

'Want to go and look for the bastards?' she said.

'No.'

9

'You can see him now,' said the voice.

'What have you done with that bloody bottle?' it added.

Pibble groaned out of his dreams. He was lying face down on the foredeck, because any other position was agony. He had not watched Dubh Artach lighthouse saunter by, banded with black and white, the waves frilling its deadly rock with twenty-foot high fluffs of foam. He had not seen in what splendours of marmalade and amethyst the Hebridean sun had sunk. His waking mind had been full of guilt for two dead men, and his sleeping mind had brimmed with pictures. Father, in his plus-twos, bringing Sir Francis, white-whiskered and querulous, saucers of brown goo: snakes of flame flaring in vacuum flasks, such as one might take to a picnic: a radio valve, and Tolerance plucking it out of its socket and saying 'Damned ironic, hey?': Mr Toger at the porch, sniffing the air and saying 'I had not imagined that you made use of money.': Mother laughing in her print dress and new hat while she tore up the rotten pyjamas because they couldn't afford the kite in the post office window: Father putting on his specs to peer by the erratic gas-light at an enormous photograph of Sir Francis Francis standing on the steps of the Stock Exchange: the rent collector passing the stained-glass in the porch, knocking at either side but never at Number 8: Sir Francis, tottering, teasing a bemedalled general by drawing from his ear, as if by magic, a sailor suit and a pair of Sunday shoes and a special shirt with lace at the cuffs: the Head pacing the dais before the school and talking, while he touched his cane lightly with the tips of his fingers, about fees: Father lying in his medicine-smelling room, listless, not explaining that the fistful of glossy conkers which Jamie had brought from the Common would be dull and wrinkled by the time it came to place them one by one into the back of the fire with the tongs on the night after the funeral, and Sir Francis snarling that that was forty-three years ago: a wallet full of clean pound notes, and Mother taking it out of Father's plus-two jacket and going off to buy the 'medicine' that made her so hazy in the evenings and snappish in the mornings: Mr Toger sniffing the air of the porch again.

Yes, thought Pibble as he came painfully to a crawling position, no chance of Mr Toger being so attentive, even to a smooth-skinned widow, if there weren't money in the house. It was almost dark.

'Want a hand?' said Dorothy.

Pibble's hurts of the morning were leagued with a thousand aches and stiffnesses that had stolen over his body during his drowsing. He tried to haul himself up by the mast, but dropped back after fitful scrabbling.

'It's OK,' he said, 'I'll crawl to him.'

'No you won't,' she said. 'That's my job.'

He heard a strange noise above his head and craned up. She was leaning her arm against the mast, swaying and chortling. He crawled to the edge of the foredeck, let his legs down over the edge and was standing in the well. Dazedly he manoeuvred himself aft, gripping the gunwale with both hands, towards the hunched shape which sat by the tiller, outlined every thirty seconds by the far flash of the lighthouse behind them. Sir Francis was wearing a souwester as if it had been a sunbonnet.

'That the peeler?' croaked the hateful voice.

'Yes, sir.'

'Sit down.'

Sitting hurt, but so did anything else. Pibble sat.

'Killed two of our brown brethren, Dorrie says.'

'They were trying to sink us by dropping rocks, but I managed to bring the helicopter down with a kite.'

'Damned idiots – couldn't even outwit *you*. Won't look too good in court, will it, Pibble?'

'There'll have to be an inquest, but I don't know how

much of what happened need come out in court. Unless somebody was watching from the lighthouse with binoculars, Dorothy's the only witness, and . . .'

'You call her Miss Machin, you damned upstart.'

'I don't imagine Miss Machin will go talking to reporters.'

'You're relying on *me* to keep her off the bottle, hey?'

Pibble was silent.

'Got me off the island, did you, Pibble?'

'As far as this, anyway.'

'Couldn't have done it without me, could you?'

'I couldn't have done it without Rita and Miss Machin, either.'

'You're an insolent damned jack-in-office, Pibble. And now you expect me to babble away about your damned father, just to show how grateful I am. I won't do it, I tell you.'

'In that case I'll tell you what I think happened, and if you want to you can tell me whether I'm right or wrong.'

Sir Francis snorted beside him in the dark.

'In about 1910,' said Pibble, 'you were trying to build bigger and better vacuum chambers to continue your work on gas plasmas. My father did the glass-blowing. I imagine you'd already done all the work for which you got your Nobel Prize, but that was only a half-way house and you wanted to go on from there.'

Sir Francis started to say something, then stopped.

'My father was intensely devoted to you and your work, and took an almost obsessive interest in it. He made theoretic suggestions which you thought impertinent, but he also tried to come up with a technical solution to the problem of finding a metal-to-glass seal which would stand the very high temperatures you were trying to work at. None of his solutions was any good, but one of them – I think it was perhaps one which involved a glue and a solidifier, like these modern resin glues – turned out later to be valuable for some other process. I imagine it was something to do with radio, and my guess is that it provided a short-cut in the mass-production of radio valves. This must have been a problem in the later stages of the war, and perhaps your work with gas plasmas meant that you did war-research on radio valves which also involve vacuums. You took out a patent on my father's double seal. Radio boomed after the war, and you made a lot of money out of it. You never did much deep theoretical research in radio – I know your atom bomb work was involved in the behaviour of the gases around the bomb in the split second after the original explosion, which looks as if professionally you had stuck to your main field. But meanwhile, more or less as a hobby, you did technical work on other radio patents which eventually made you a very rich man indeed. Some time after the first war my father might have seen your name in the paper not in connection with your theoretical work but in connection with being rich from the profits on a radio valve seal. He came to see you. I think he wanted a job like his old one, but you'd got past having to depend on one man to make your apparatus, and you thought he'd be a nuisance, so you bought him off. I think you probably bought our house in Clapham for us, and perhaps that you provided us later with some sort of pension, because we seem to have been erratically comfortable and poor . . .'

'I've been poor too,' said Sir Francis irritably. 'Damned poor. And it was worse for me because I knew what it was like not to be poor, knew what it was like to have two ponies, and my own groom to keep them, and our own stream to fish – I could see the willows over it from my nursery window – and a floorful of parcels to open on my birthday. And then my idiot dad went bust for his otter-hounds, and I had to go to a second-rate school and a second-rate college and work with the sons of clerks and colonials, yes, squabble with forty of them for the use of the only damned footpump in the laboratory. I've had to scrape and save to pay Everett ten shillings for a glass-blowing lesson. I've had to crawl to mechanics to get them to turn me a couple of inches of brass tubing a fortnight later. I've had to trudge down to the Cavendish on a Sunday and let myself in to the stink of gas and battery acid, because I couldn't pay some mechanic to keep my vacuums up till Monday. Why d'you think I know these waters? Because it was the cheapest holiday a man could take. I can

178

remember three whole years when I felt sick to be in the same room as Jeans, with his rich American wife and his estate at Dorking. Jeans floated off in his damned motor while I slogged back to my digs on a rusty bicycle through the dust and stink he left behind him.'

'And then you were rich again,' said Pibble.

'And then I was rich again. I ought never to have had to be poor.'

'But you gave it all away.'

'What do you want me to do? It was my damned money, and yet I was supposed to die smiling and let a chicken-hearted government dribble it away mollycoddling the mob, or on some useless dead-end of aeronautics. It began with stopping a leak, hey, so why should it end by becoming one? Soon as I'm dead it's all a waste anyway, but I'm damned well going to see it wasted my way.'

'How much was the Nobel Prize worth in 1912?'

'None of your business. Enough to let me off coming up here for my holidays, not enough to make me free. Plenty of offers of jobs, mind you, but not an extra penny at the Cavendish, and that was where I had to stay, mucking in at J.J.'s deadly dull tea-parties in the Preparation Room – "You are to talk shop," he used to boom at us – *me!*'

'Why did you have to stay?'

'If you weren't a total illiterate you'd know that the work I got my Prize for was never finished. We couldn't build the damned apparatus. They've done it since, with millions to spend, twenty years after I tried. Those days the only place I had a hope of building the gadgets I needed was the Cavendish, unless you're asking me to go and live among the apes in America. I stayed, and went to tea-parties, and talked shop, and waited for your damned dad to come up with an answer.'

'And he never did.'

Sir Francis snorted in the whistling dark.

'I take it the contract's off,' said Pibble at last.

'Twasn't a contract. 'Twasn't even a scrap of paper.'

Pibble could *hear* him grinning.

'Perhaps not,' he said. 'I've noticed that, however much you've concealed, all you've told me has been the truth, with two exceptions . . .'

'Hey?'

'You laughed when I told you my father had been a ticket-clerk, which you must have known. And you said you never met my mother.'

'You're a fool, Pibble. I always laugh at the notion of your dad helping puffing cockneys to catch their trains, and I said that he never told me about your mum. He didn't either. She did.'

'Oh. Well, then, you also said that you'd tell me everything you could remember about my father provided I got you off the island.'

'You didn't get me off, you impertinent numbskull. I got you off. Where'd you have been without me?'

'I could ask the same, sir.'

'If you hadn't come busybodying north, Pibble, d'you think those boobies in brown would have monkeyed about with my cortisone, hey? But for you, I'd have been sitting in my own room now, happy as a flea in your armpit, instead of dying of cold in this damned dull bit of ocean.'

'They'd bought the chalk to fake your pills with before they knew about me. Besides, you asked me to come.'

'Can't an old man indulge his fancy without every snivelling peeler trying to hold him to it?'

'I shan't try to hold you to anything, sir.'

'I'd think not! Only got to tell your masters what you did to that damned helicopter, haven't I, hey?'

'I'll have to put in a report on that myself.'

The old man snorted and sat silent. He loosed a painful few inches of sail. At last he snorted again.

'Ninety-two years!' he yelled. 'Time enough to get used to idiots, you'd think. And so I have, so I have. But high-minded idiots give me the itch still. You want me to tell you that this rigmarole of yours is historical truth, hey?'

'It doesn't matter,' said Pibble. 'You told me that the man who sent you the cutting with my name in it was malicious, so I'm fairly sure that something happened between you and my father, and that other people in the scientific world know about it. One day it will come out, but that doesn't interest me. Even supposing I did have some claim on you I wouldn't make it. All I want to be told is what my father was like and why he finished as he did. I can't force you to tell me what happened, and I wouldn't try. You said I was a blackmailer, like my family – that's another point – but if you don't want to tell me you needn't.'

'Damned rum thing, heredity,' grumbled Sir Francis. 'Your dad was the doggiest man I ever knew, always hanging around with appealing eyes waiting to have his ego scratched, and now his son tracks me down, snuffling across fifty years of my life, and does the same.'

'The dog it was that died,' said Pibble.

'Hey?'

'I'm sorry, my mind's wandering. There was a dog on the island. Its name was Love. It hunted me. I think it's dead now.'

'Down the arches of the years, hey? Damned soppy ode, if ever I read one. Go and get a riding-light.'

The women were both asleep, Dorothy snoring on a sail, Rita almost toppling off the hummock of canvas. When Pibble tried to ease her to a safer position she slid into his tired arms, bubbling soft unarticulated murmurs between barely open lips. He lowered her to the dank floor and readjusted the sails to make a nest for her. She clung to him, heavy and cloying, while he worked her up the slope and settled her in; he had to wriggle out of her grasp before he could cover her with a loose fold of sail. Ashamed, he tousled the top of her head as one might a sleeping child's. She frowned. He got the green riding-light out of a locker and lit it from the red one.

There was nowhere to hang it in the stern so Pibble settled on the bottom boards, where its surreal light turned Sir Francis's crimson visage black and made the corners of his eyes glint green, like a Venusian's. He was folding a piece of paper over.

'Sit down and look at this,' he croaked.

He poised the paper just out of reach, so that the light caught its surface. A line of his own strong script ran across the top. Below that, with the characteristic curled and finnicky upright at the beginning of the W, but very shaky

181

from there on, came the words 'Willoughby Pibble'; below them, peasant-sturdy, 'Mabel Pibble'.

'What is it?' said their son. 'Why do you carry it about with you.'

'Course I don't carry it about with me,' said the old man. 'It a'n't that important. Looked it out when I heard you'd come. We've finished with it now, though, hey?'

Pibble had been staring at the paper with the timeless numbness of a gardener leaning on his fork and staring into a bonfire. He moved too late when the old claw let go. He clutched as the scrap swirled forward, past him, dipped at the gunwale, rose again and dipped into the hissing blackness beyond the boat. He flung himself to the side and held the lantern high – there it was, white and square, dipping down the lurch of a wave, so clear a mark that it might have been tossed overboard to measure the speed at which they were sailing, four feet away, a world out of reach. He watched it go, then returned painfully to his place.

'You killed him,' he said.

'Hey?'

'Twice.'

'Poppycock! He'd have gone off to fight whatever I'd said. He was that sort.'

'When he was very ill my mother sent for you. That's when you saw the house and he looked for the bit of ring on your watch-chain. You didn't want to be bothered any more. I don't know what the paper said, I imagine that they both signed an agreement not to molest you any more, and that in return for this you guaranteed to pay my mother a pension after my father was dead, enough to educate me and for us both to live on. But there's no reason for you not to show it to me if you hadn't worded it in such a way that you knew he'd have no interest in living after that. My mother wouldn't have realised. I went into his room to show him some conkers that evening.'

'Most embarrassing thing I can remember in my whole life,' said Sir Francis, 'is my dad crying after he'd put one of his damned dogs down. Always did it himself. Wouldn't let the huntsmen do it. Now I've done a lot for you in your life, Pibble, and you're just beginning to see it. I'll do something more, and a damned sight more useful than drivelling on about the past. Put your hand under mine and I'll show you how to get the best out of a boat. That's something worth knowing.'

The mittened hand was cold as stone, but firm and certain. Beneath its guidance Pibble learnt the feel of the sea, and the tiny adjustments of the tiller by which it is possible to present the keel to the water so that the element accepts the intruder without irritability. When he got it right he found the relationship curiously exhilarating.

'You'll do,' said the old voice at last. 'You'll never be good, but you'll do. Now you can take us back to Oban. I shan't have to tell you twice, shall I, seeing how you treasure up every scrap of nonsense that falls from my lips.'

Dazedly Pibble listened to instructions about lights and islands. They were heading northeast up the Firth of Lorne, and Oban lay near the top on the right-hand side. Only three sets of lights really mattered, and he contrived to fix their names and meanings somehow amid the chaos of his mind.

'Right,' said Sir Francis. 'When you see the Lady Rock light distinctly nearer to the light on the left-hand side of the sound of Mull, you can look right and you'll see another light on your right-hand side. You lash the tiller in place and go and fetch Dorrie. She'll show you how to tack to and fro till I'm ready to take you in. Don't try and sail in yourself, or you'll run us onto Kerrera like the fool you are. Got it?'

'Yes, sir.'

'Well, stop sitting there like a drowned hedgehog and go and get Dorrie. She can take me in and wrap me up, and then she'd better get some sleep. I'll need her at Oban.'

'Why did you send for me?'

'To get me and my book off this island before the brown boobies got their claws into it. Wrote forty damned dull letters, all the same, and put yours in with them. Knew they wouldn't open more than two or three.'

'I mean why *me*?'

'Who else was there, you prize oaf? Go and get Dorrie.'

Yes, thought Pibble, groping painfully forward, who else was there? Only one man had ever really loved the old terror, so he had sent for his son. And then betrayed him – as the scorpion in the sick fable betrays the frog that is ferrying it over the river. He *knew* the monks were opening his letters.

Dorothy was sunk in stupor, but Rita lay awake.

'I hope you've slept well, countess,' he said.

Patrician disdain flashed from her eye and arched her nostril. He could see that she might well be a connection of the Howards.

'His Majesty has done me the honour of raising me to the rank and dignity of Marchioness,' she said.

'Congratulations.'

'In my own right.'

'That's nice.'

'It distresses me much, sir, to learn that you are not His Majesty's true heir.'

'Oh. Well. Anyway, His Majesty would be grateful if you would help him back to the cabin now.'

'I am his to command.'

She rose from the canvas and sped into the dark, balancing without trouble against the lurch of the boat. Pibble stumbled after her.

'Brought the loony,' shouted Sir Francis. 'Where's Dorrie?'

'Miss Machin's asleep. I hear, Sire, that you have raised our passenger to the rank and dignity of Marchioness, in her own right. Also that it is now learnt that I am not Your Majesty's true heir.'

Sir Francis laughed.

'Rum do,' he croaked at last. 'If I'd my time over again I'd do a few years' work on second sight. Time somebody sorted it out, hey? You take the tiller, Pibble, and do your damndest not to drown us. Lend me your arm, m'lady.'

It was a dreary night. Under Pibble's unguided hand the boat became oafish again, but in these smaller waves it mattered less. The dark shore of Mull seemed barely to change its shape, but imperceptibly they worked up the long funnel of water that pierces to the heart of Scotland. The Garvalloch lighthouse neared, its blink flicking below the black curve of the sail. Sir Francis was due out again

soon after that, and Pibble dreaded having to face him
again. But he didn't come. The Firth narrowed. The waves
changed their shape as the tide turned. The night wheeled
on. An hour before time he lashed the tiller into place and
went to wake Dorothy. Rita was crouched on the floor,
asleep, her head in the old man's lap; the crooked hand
drifted to and fro through her glossy locks. Dorothy was
snoring, but sat up the moment he shook her, glanced at the
unlikely lovers, sniffed and followed him out.

'The bottle's in the tin which had the kite in it,' he said.

'Ta.'

'D'you mind if I talk to you?'

'Carry on.'

He told her what he'd told Sir Francis. He was concerned
to make it sound as real as possible, because he'd never tell
anyone again.

'What did Frank say?' she said when he'd finished.

'Nothing either way.'

'Then you're not far off. If you'd been wrong, he couldn't
have borne not to tell you what an idiot you are. Have a
drink before I scoff the lot.'

He took a small mouthful from the bottle and handed it
back to her. She'd got through the equivalent of about six
doubles while he'd been talking.

'What are you going to do?' she said.

'Nothing.'

'He's a sod,' she said, 'and he will be till he dies. Anything homosexual between him and your father, d'you
think?'

'No,' said Pibble, unmoved. 'Evidently my father adored
him, and I think he felt some sort of regard and affection for
my father. My father gave him half a gold ring in 1914, and
he carried it on his watch-chain for fifty years.'

'So that's what that was,' said Dorothy. 'Blast, I've got
the hiccups. I tell you what I think – his mother died when
he was born, his father was a clod, none of us whores were
any more to him than rubber women at night and servant-
gals by day, but your father was something else, like that bit
in *Alice* where she has to get down on the floor to peek
along the passage into the garden she can't get into because

185

she's too big. He knew he'd missed something he ought to have had, and he couldn't bear it. And it frightened him, too, I bet, the idea of anyone having a sort of claim on him he couldn't pay off. I know Frank.'

'He bought my father off in the end.'

'Only by the money part of it. Pardon me. The other part of it's been fretting him all his life, like a boil on the back of your neck you can't help fingering.'

'I get the impression,' said Pibble, 'that when he first came to Clumsey Island he took the Community's ideas rather more seriously than he does now. He told me he got to know the jargon well at one time.'

'What the hell's that got to do with it?'

'Well, I think his conscious motive for coming was to get away from reporters and to evade taxes, both of which he managed. But here were this lot who in a mad sort of way stood for the same things as my father stood for. He was a bit unworldly, and he was certainly a good man. These people were extremely unworldly, and claimed to ·be immeasurably virtuous. Possibly the sheer exaggeration of their claims seemed – well, you talked about Alice's door – they may have seemed for a bit to offer a door big enough for someone Sir Francis's size to go through.'

'You just can't tell with the old bastard,' said Dorothy. 'But he didn't stay holy long. He knew it was crap, and didn't mind saying so. But when that old Professor wallah sent him the newspaper cutting about you, the boil started to itch again and he couldn't resist picking it. But he was still scared. He wanted to *feel* that he couldn't trust you. He *wanted* you to be acting from dirty motives, and that would prove, pardon me, that would prove, oh, Christ, where was I?'

'It would prove that the door was never there at all and so he hadn't missed anything.'

Mysteriously Dorothy started to sob in the dark, hiccuping between the sobs. Suddenly she said 'How much further do we have to go up this bloody lake?'

Guiltily Pibble looked about him. Three lights, evenly spaced, shone on the left, and two more close together on the right.

'We're supposed to go to and fro here until he comes out again,' he said. 'Unless you feel competent to steer us into Oban Harbour. That's it, over there.'

'Not bloody likely,' she said.

So there was an hour's meaningless work, tracing a half-mile triangle round and round in the Firth. Pibble fetched the gnawed remains of the loaf from the cabin and bit at it dry-mouthed. At last a strange cry, like the mating call of some goose, rose from the bows. Without a word Dorothy staggered aft, helped the hunched bundle of spiteful genius across the netting, and took her bottle up to the foredeck. Sir Francis looked about him, snorted, took the tiller out of Pibble's hand and steered for the twin light.

'Going back to catch a few pick-pockets now?' he snarled.

'Yes.'

'Forget the whole thing, hey?'

'If I can.'

'There's some sense, even in a numbskull.'

They didn't exchange another word during the long reach south. Sir Francis snapped out orders for the two tacks that took them into the narrow sound, but Dorothy did the work, singing *Smoke Gets in your Eyes* and hiccupping between lines. She had a rather pleasant light tenor.

Lights blazed on the quay, and voices clamoured. Two launches creamed out. A searchlight glared. Pibble could see the ambulance now, and the squad of journalists, and the film cameras, and more lights flicking on as the generators boomed.

'Ahoy!' called a loudspeaker from the larger launch, 'Is Sir Francis Francis aboard?'

'Yes,' shouted Pibble.

The other launch raced beyond them and closed in like a coursing greyhound on its hare. A camera crew stood tense on the bucketing prow.

'Get the mainsail down, you buffoon,' called Sir Francis.

Pibble worked the winch and it fell, flapping; he heaved and clawed its nail-tearing hardness into a quiet heap. The boat drifted towards the quay with exquisitely judged slowness. A dozen reporters, notebooks and tape-recorders at the ready, were poised for the jump. Pibble summoned his last gill of authority.

'Keep off, all of you!' he shouted. 'We're coming ashore!'

There was a mild thud, which almost tossed Dorothy overboard where she stood swaying in the bows, but she clutched at the forestay, steadied, and with a wild gesture threw a coil of rope into the middle of the mob. It caught a man with a microphone full in the face and became entangled with his wires, but somebody made it fast. Sir Francis shouted and pointed with his stick at another coil in the stern, so Pibble picked that up and threw it on to the quay. It tautened jerkily.

There were four rusted iron rungs to climb up the sea-slimed stone, and Sir Francis took two minutes to manage them, snarling like a hurt bitch at the officious arms that tried to help him. He turned at the top and shouted down.

'You! Pibble! Bring my parcel.'

It lay on the lockers in the cabin. He picked it up and then shook Rita by the shoulder. She woke, sat up and recoiled from his touch all in one movement.

'We've arrived,' he said, wishing that he could have kept the sourness out of his voice.

Head high, without thanks, she stalked across the netting and climbed the ladder. At the top she hesitated, bewildered by the glare of the crowd, long enough for Pibble to hoist himself up beside her; then she swooped across the cobbles to nestle against the old scarecrow. A flurry of flashlights popped, in whose spasmodic glare she looked like a Millais heroine in an electric storm, serene and pale and not long for this world. Sir Francis grabbed her to him, grinning, and with delighted rudeness answered the questions flung at him by the scum of the earth.

Pibble watched the scene from the top of the ladders, turning the parcel over and over in his hands, feeling the flexible weight of that exquisitely penned manuscript under the brown paper. Suppose he were to drop it in the harbour, quietly now while no one was watching him: the salt and oil would soak through to obliterate all that spite and pride, and Sir Francis alone would know that it wasn't an accident, as he, Pibble, alone knew what had happened to Father. That would be a just punishment, surely . . .

As he turned the manuscript over yet again an arm was flung with clumsy affection round his shoulder. Dorothy, reeking of garlic and whisky, lurched against him and brandished the empty bottle at the bright-lit tumult.

'Don't know who the real bloody hero is, do they?' she shouted.

Her cry came in a lull of babble, and several heads turned. A question was asked. He detached himself from Dorothy and tucked the manuscript safely under his arm. In the near silence Sir Francis's voice creaked on, clear and unmelodious as the clack of a roosting pheasant.

' . . . and then he damned near drowned us all,' he was saying. 'I knew his father. He was a busybody, too.'

MYSTERIOUS PRESS—

the exciting new crime imprint from Arrow Books

☐ A CAST OF KILLERS	Sidney Kirkpatrick	£2.95
☐ ROUGH CIDER	Peter Lovesey	£2.50
☐ WEXFORD: AN OMNIBUS	Ruth Rendell	£5.95
☐ WOLF TO THE SLAUGHTER	Ruth Rendell	£2.50
☐ KILL ZONE	Loren Estleman	£2.50
☐ MOONSPENDER	Jonathan Gash	£2.50
☐ HARE SITTING UP	Michael Innes	£2.50
☐ THE JUNKYARD DOG	Robert Campbell	£2.50
☐ THE COST OF SILENCE	Margaret Yorke	£2.50
☐ THE GONDOLA SCAM	Jonathan Gash	£2.50
☐ PEARLHANGER	Jonathan Gash	£2.50